S0-FER-047

Dear Writer's Relief Team,

Thank you so much for all the hard work you do to help the writers. Most stories in this book were edited at your office. Thank you for your dedication to excellence!

Maria Logden

Maria Logven

# THE CELL OF A SOUL

New York

authorHOUSE®

*AuthorHouse™*
*1663 Liberty Drive, Suite 200*
*Bloomington, IN 47403*
*www.authorhouse.com*
*Phone: 1-800-839-8640*

*© 2008 Maria Logven. All rights reserved.*

*No part of this book may be reproduced, stored in a retrieval system, or transmitted by any means without the written permission of the author.*

*First published by AuthorHouse 10/24/2008*

*ISBN: 978-1-4343-9996-0 (sc)*
*ISBN: 978-1-4343-8660-1 (hc)*

*Printed in the United States of America*
*Bloomington, Indiana*

*This book is printed on acid-free paper.*

*"Trapped in Love" appeared in Diner November 2007*
*"Childhood Story Revised" appeared in Sofa Ink Quarterly January 2008*

***Illustrated by Michael Cheval***

# Contents

# S-Story

I SIT DOWN TO A KEYBOARD, and my fingers submerge into the deep thick of forest. They glide inside through the wet green of pine needles until I touch the bottom. My fingertips dig into the coolness of melting snow and into the warmth of breathing fur, for it is early spring, and the Bear is still asleep. On the S-key, for she lives in my S-Story, the Bear slept through the winter, and nothing disturbed her S-Sleep.

On the A-key to the left, Ariel, the airy spirit incarcerated in a cloven pine, groans in his prison ever more restless. As the S-Spring gains strength, warm and gentle Z-Zephyr replaces the chills of winter's winds. It travels up from the Z-key to circle around the cloven pine and release Ariel into its airy texture. Together they take off flying and make the S-Spring true, for Ariel within Zephyr is a breath of spring.

Flying east, flying west, Ariel remembers his neighbor, the Bear, whose S-Sleep prison is so similar to his own. It is time for the Bear to break free and join the merriment of the season. Ariel tickles her nose with falling pine needles and pulls on her long, brown fur. But the

Bear will not move. Then, Ariel orders the grand Mount Everest that stands wide and proud up on the E-key to send down clouds from the sky. The S-key fills with floating, milky-white shapes, and Ariel flies his Zephyr to crowd clouds around the Bear.

A great roar rolls through the keyboard, shaking each key with its creatures. The Bear opens her eyes to see her Dear. The D-Dear Bear is roaring restless, for he did not sleep through the winter but roamed around the keyboard, hunting. He knows it all, he has pressed all the keys, him, the wise traveler, so Dear.

He saw it all, except for this, the Bear among the clouds. Sleepy and fresh, she invites him in, onto her S-key S-story. He steps inside and together, they bathe in the gentle air of spring. Cuddling in the pillowy clouds, they converse with Ariel. Zephyr lifts them up to the zenith of Everest and returns them back to the keyboard.

S-Summer replaces S-Spring, but the S-Story continues. The Bear and Dear play hide-and-seek in the clouds. A wonderful game, except that the Bear is always the one searching. They dine on wild strawberries, raspberries, and blueberries. One day Dear says that he never felt this way, never knew this comfort of closeness, this tranquility of quiet happiness. The Bear ponders, for she thinks they are being pretty loud.

They play hide-and-seek as usual, but the Bear cannot find her Dear. She searches and searches among the clouds. He must have discovered a new hiding place. Where, where? He had a wonderful time, but the one who tasted blood cannot feed long on berries. Her Dear is too restless for forever, too free for together. Where, where? He fled her S-Story like Ariel, who escaped the cloven pine, like she who awoke from the confines of sleep. Where, where? The Bear searches. Deceptive clouds of spring! Take them away, Ariel, up to the sky where they belong. The Bear wants clarity to find her Dear. Zephyr chases away the clouds and leaves with Ariel for other keys, faraway P-Places in lovely L-Lands.

Where, where? The Bear searches. No more clouds and nowhere to hide her embarrassment, her sorrow. Where, where? No S-Spring or S-Summer in her S-Story. Clouds are unreachably high in the sky. Did she ever touch them, him? Was it not a beautiful, impossible dream?

Barrenness. The Bear can leave the S-key and start searching the faraway P-Places in lovely L-Lands, but she must learn to hunt for survival or starve. Or she can stay and sleep.

When the Dear leaves, great heaviness bears down on the Bear. W-Winter descends into my S-Story, and I sleep though the changing seasons, adding year by year to the still-life painting of my Bear.

W-Winter offers me time to W-Write, but the sleeping Bear bears the S-key of my keyboard down. This affects my S-Style and makes everything I compose resemble the S-Story. Constants vary from one story to another, but the variables remain constant—each story is solving for the X, for the missing Dear, who once escaped from my S-Story.

MICHAEL CHEVAL 2007

# *Trapped in Love*

## Foreword

Sunday. Moon years passed since our breakup. My spring bubble messages to you went unanswered, leaving me to attempt this new form of communication.

I imagine staying over at your place for a night of wine and kisses. I will take your hand and tell you that it has ten fingers because the in-between fingers count too. I will trace your in-between fingers with my tongue and then suck the real ones. You will fit your real fingers into my in-betweens and I will read you my story, our hands clasped into a lovers' fist.

But if the impossible is not on your syllabus, take my story then, and read it alone as I embrace the fantasy in another empty bedroom.

## Moon Virgins

Monday. I stay at work until dark. Walking through the rotating door, I bump into the warm darkness face to face. Out on the street I raise my eyes to the black, moon-filled sky. Thousands of bright and yellow full-moon disks are moving rapidly along their intricate paths governed by complex gravity relationships with Earth and each other. The moons chase after moons, collide with moons, bounce off the moons, coalesce, break up.

Many scientists devoted their lives to the study of moon behaviors. Many artists explored through various mediums the aesthetics of the ever-changing glowing forms that the moons create against the black sky background. Just recently a young artist produced a five-second film where the moons shaped a perfect heart, which was bombarded by a straight line of moons resembling an arrow. This little flick created much scandalous commotion. Some insisted that instead of being blessed with miraculous luck to be the witness and the capturer of an ephemeral image, the artist possessed a rare gift of audacity to lie and defend his lie with outrageous probity before the audience of millions. Others believed that the heart image was a special sign and the artist was meant to spread the enigmatic message, perhaps of warning or blessing.

The artist's girlfriend claimed that she was with him and saw it all with her own eyes. It was his habit to spend three hours each night in the Park filming the sky, as if he always knew that one day a miracle would happen; he just had to wait for it. To avoid distraction, he never allowed the girlfriend to go with him until that night when she cried and begged and declared that he kept her away from his life and she would leave unless he took her with him. He gave in and that night a miracle happened. The girlfriend, however, believed that the heart they saw was a message for them and them alone. She was deeply hurt by the artist distributing the film to the masses and making a million-dollar fortune off it. She broke up with him, but called him every night. According to rumors, they will be getting married soon.

I walk through the dark streets, usually empty by this hour, and gaze at the sky. The continuous, rapid commotion of yellow circles fills me with energy, a special excitement, as if there is much movement in my life, as if something big is about to happen.

I almost never see moons forming any shapes, at least not distinct ones. I don't look for that. Instead, I play the virgin game. I pick out the moon and designate it to be a virgin. Then I follow it with my eyes until it bumps into another moon, at which point it loses its virginity. It's very exciting to watch how my moon heads for another but misses it by what looks like a few centimeters. Or how it runs away from one moon just to smash into another by accident, in the effort to escape. If the collision results in two moons combining into a larger single one—that is a marriage. If they bounce off each other—that's a broken heart. I wonder, what is the probability of two moons bouncing off each other but then meeting and merging together, like the artist and his girlfriend.

I can play this game for hours, walking down the street in no particular direction but usually finding myself in the Park. I followed the paths of many moons, but however long they last, each one loses its virginity eventually. The thought comforts me.

## Lip Biting

I am biting my lips. It is kind of a problem for me, which started awhile back, but I chose to ignore it for a long time. I bite my lips when I need to concentrate at work. Bite them when I am uneasy or anxious before meetings. Bite them in the train when I am bored on my way home.

Thankfully, I find myself in a place and time where all sorts of medicines are available to treat unpleasant habits. Today I acquired my medicine and want to try it out. It is strange to will myself into lip biting. Usually it occurs naturally, without my knowing my tongue, which searches inquisitively across the skin to find the area of smoothness, one that is the most healed, in order to sink my teeth into it. I will myself into biting and immediately feel your lips touching mine, softly but distinctly enough. I worried that it would feel fake or too vague to recognize. But the medicine is perfect: your lips are wonderful.

This treatment is meant to be a pleasant, private reminder that will always prompt me to stop hurting myself until I learn not to. Whether lost in thought or inundated by emotions, a tender sensation of a kiss would make me aware of my tongue and tooth action.

I look out the train window at the bright yellow moons circling and chasing one another across the dark sky. Again I bite my lip, this time harder, and your kiss follows promptly. The light scent of blood in my mouth. I feel myself the happiest woman on Earth heading home after a long day at work, moon spheres shining at me as I accept your kisses, one after another, as many as I want, as many as I can bite out of my lips.

## Green Mermaid

I am miserable alone in my bed. The thought of thinking of you frightens me and pains. That's why I turn into a mermaid. Not the redheaded one from cartoons who is full of love and life. I become a real mermaid, with green seaweed hair and a cold fish tail down from my waist, not a true woman anymore. How do mermaids reproduce anyway? They are always created but never born, is my answer.

I lie on the bottom of a pond, motionless. I open my eyes to look at hazy circles on the pond surface caused by my rare breathing. I close my eyes again. Move my tail and feel the swirl of water around my body, wait for it to settle down. There is nothing more to life. The mermaid cannot be happy or sad. She is just a part of the pond's green, like the seaweed inside it and the forest around it. If drunken men, a group of loud kids, or merry lovers would come upsetting my peace, I'd drown them to make them quiet. I cannot be disturbed.

With my eyes closed, I listen. A pleasant sound of a leaf falling onto the surface from the nearby tree. A cry of a night bird from afar. Quiescence.

My vision fluctuates. I am frightened by its reality. Missing you is safer. I bite my lips and fall asleep with your kisses.

## Saloon Design and Management

Tuesday. Early in the morning I take the train to work. A few years ago an eccentric millionaire had an idea of turning train cars into social saloons. He put much money into the experiment that proved more successful than was initially expected. The idea caught on, heavily supported by large corporations that considered the project as part of their work-life balance program.

On her way to work, a young mother boards the Parenthood train car, where she can drink morning tea and share her concerns with other young mothers and a trained professional serving as a host. Businessmen board the Business News car to discuss the latest market trends and meet with leading economists over coffee. Arts & Theater Daily advertises and reviews current events one might wish to attend in the evening. A Painting a Day focuses on a single work of art—its interpretation and significance in history. The Media car carries movie star fans, who gossip about latest scandals. In the Shop Smart car, the hosts advertise popular stores. In Dream Vacations, travel companies highlight their vacation packages.

Each train has a standard selection of saloons and a few devoted to special interests for fishers, physicists, astrologists, and many others. Saloons that prove to be unpopular are replaced by others. To create a new saloon, one has to submit a proposal signed by at least two hundred passengers who'd support the idea.

Much careful planning goes into saloon design and theme selection. Every train needs to present a large variety of popular theme cars. Every car has to satisfy the interest of as many passengers as possible. Hosts must be sure that everyone in their car feels welcomed and entertained. Plenty of research books are written on this topic, which is now a popular university major—Saloon Design and Management.

Today I do not wish to talk or to listen. I board the Quiet car, where passengers usually read, listen to their players, or sleep. I take a seat near the window and watch the passing outside.

## Itching

By the end of the day at work, my hand starts to itch but I cannot find the exact spot, so I scratch all over. It itches anyway, as if there is more to my body than I can see, as if the source of itching is a part of my hand that occupies another dimension.

I also discover a thin red line down my wrist on a safe distance from the center. I know I didn't do it. I hope there is no other dimension of me that I am not aware of.

## Spring Bubbles

When I say I sense spring,
it means the air is warm enough
and contains enough pollen
to sustain a population of bubbles.

They float around with the wind
but often gather above large flower areas
or under flowering tree branches
where the pollen is most abundant.

They absorb pollen to keep their
membranes strong and glowing
with fuchsia, violet, teal, olive, lime,
aqua, gold, sea, or sunrise colors.

Large quantities of pollen powder
must be consumed by their
thin, transparent circumferences
that average 10 cm in diameter.

It is always a joy to come across
a merry meadow with a herd
of grazing spring bubbles kissing
flower petals for more sweet pollen.

It is a pleasant tingly surprise
whenever a spring bubble brushes
against your hand, cheek or shoulder
as the warm breeze carries it by.

If you are lucky, you know the delightfully
keen sensation of tiny bubble droplets
showering your mood with spring freshness
when the bubble breaks against your skin.

I have a unique secret experience to share—
once I walked right into the giant bubble,
few inches taller than me and much much wider.
It was right before I saw you for the first time.

**Spring Bubbles**

Thousands of moon years ago, I took a creative writing class. The assignment was to write a personal reality poem. This poem is one of very few that I am proud to have written. It stands out in my memory among thousands of concepts that I tried to convey in thousand words in thousand poems. I enjoy it. Not for the language or content that I put into its crafting, but for the perception that it gave me. There isn't a spring that does not remind me of Spring Bubbles.

As I take my late-evening walk after work, I recall the poem. Even in the dark I can discern colorful bubbles crowding in the grass below blooming trees. When I walk by a large group, a red bubble separates from the rest and follows me, circling around my feet. What does it want from me, I wonder. Maybe I should stop and take a closer look. Perhaps it carries a message for me from a secret admirer. From you, I want to get a message from you. I know it is impossible. You do not like my romantic, sentimental ways. You would never approve of my poem if I ever let you read it. You would never consider sending me a message in a red spring bubble. Color red stands for passion; it also stands for "stop." I am bad at interpreting symbols.

## A Tree

I head toward the Park playing the virgin game with yellow moons, the red spring bubble still circling my feet. I enter the green Meadow of Sorrow and stop to gaze into a tree. There are many trees framing the meadow and this one is no larger or stranger. It is tall enough, straight enough, thin enough, but it stands out to my eyes like the shape of a lover in a crowded street. Slowly I come closer and lean my head against the trunk, my blond lock of hair caught and curled in hard branches.

There once was a man, a lover of many women. A man with passion for the brilliant, complex, ingenious. A master himself, he enjoyed the mastery in others. The mundane bored him. Once the last of the fireworks sparks disappeared into the night sky, he had no interest in walking his lady home or shopping or meeting parents or inspiring occasion for more fireworks. He would look around for some other display of color, drawn to it with honest intensity, devoting himself, giving himself fully to a new cause. He refused closeness and knew no warmth in return. Most women he left kept a part of him and as the thousand moon years went by, he hardened into a tree.

I hug the tree trunk close to my body. It was always like this—you never hugged me back, having left your hugging to some other woman of the past. You did kiss me, though. And I took kissing away from you.

That happened yesterday, during a Monday lunch. On my insistence, we met for a goodbye kiss in the Park, on the meadow to be known as a green Meadow of Sorrow. I remember your shape by the tree as I came closer. You touched my hair. You kissed me, and I kept it. I lied when I thought I wanted it as a medicine to cure my lip biting. I simply wanted it.

## A Kiss

I sit down and lean against the tree. It was a mistake to think that I can let go and never see you again. I will always be coming back to the tree, circling around it. With my arms holding the trunk, I hug that which is you, the ephemeral you that is so hard to grasp in the midst of the excitement and brilliance that you surround yourself with. Once I got a glimpse at you when you were yawning. There was another time when we both looked into the mirror at each other naked. The brilliance of you I enjoy, but it's the you that I love and cannot let go.

I consider turning my life into a continuous, colorful display of fireworks that would get your attention and hold it until I burn out completely. I am tired now.

I feel something tender touch my cheek. The spring bubble breaks against my skin, tickling me with drops of sweet freshness—a kiss. You did send me a message in a spring bubble. Maybe I am all wrong about you.

## Frog Witch

Later this night at home, I discover the true source of itching as I undress before sleep. It is time for my annual spring allergy breakout. My arms and legs are covered with red, watery blisters effusing fluids that harden into a greenish crust. The itch is unbearable. I close my eyes to see the green. I am sitting on a log of a dead tree, swimming slowly through the large pond framed all around by mighty woods. My legs are submerged in thick water. Itching frogs bulge out of my feet and burp, sending putrid bubbles up to the surface. The cold rain starts to dribble, covering my body with goose bumps and more frogs.

I feel a new one swelling out of my shoulder. I touch it with my finger to relieve the itch but it only grows worse, and I scratch the skin apart to reveal the wet and sticky green of the frog. It stares at me for a few moments, then opens its wide mouth to burp poisons into the air.

As the dragonfly flies past me, I turn my shoulder to let the frog burp on it. The dragonfly falls dead onto the pond surface. I pick it up and feed it to the shoulder frog that swallows and itches a little less. I look around for more insects.

## Rainbow Eyebrows

Wednesday. Sleepy in the morning, I walk across the train station waving away men with flyers advertising new themes for cars. One of them wants me to sign a proposal for The Insect World. I give him a look and walk away.

Inside Quiet train saloon, I settle into my yesterday's seat. Staring out the window makes me concentrate on the itching, so I look around in search of distraction. There is a reading man a few seats away. In a state of oblivion, he does not raise his eyes to see which stations we pass and what people come in. He is unaware of my presence and I can openly study his features. I've never seen anyone read this way. His lively, intelligent face is animated with the book's content. I watch closely as his eyebrows raise rainbow high, his eyes light up with bright colors, his mouth smiles a reversed rainbow that would almost shape a circle if it was connected with the eyebrow edges. Then the rainbow eyebrows fall and the line of his lips straightens until he smiles again.

I imagine myself involved with this man, walking his rainbow eyebrows to see where they lead me. He is about your age, which is moon years away from me. He likes to read and so do you. I note the title of his book before it's my stop to get off.

## The Meeting

Missed phone calls are the first thing I note as I come near my desk at work. There are three of them, unfamiliar number, no voicemail left. I have an away message so the caller should have known he was dialing my number. Why would he be calling so late when I wouldn't be at work to pick up? The calls were made around the time when I was in the Park, receiving a message in a spring bubble. I hope it was you. I know it is impossible.

No time to dwell on this. I grab a notebook and run to an early-morning departmental meeting. I enter the room full of my co-workers, smiling, knowing that my frogs are safely hidden from all prying eyes under a carefully selected outfit. But once the meeting starts, I have difficulty concentrating on the manager's long, monotonous speech about ongoing projects. I can feel itching frogs burp under my clothes and hope the thick material muffles their sound. At home I sprayed a lot of perfume on myself to beat the frog smell. It was different when we were together. I could enjoy work when I knew I'd see you in the evening.

I am exhausted from the night of hunting for insects to feed the frogs and ease the itching. The frog witch was a beautiful fairy once. Only a patient, loving prince can reverse the spell. He will have to bring butterflowers to the pond each night for many nights, without expecting anything in return. The witch will feed butterflowers to her frogs until they satiate and stop itching. The spell will be broken and the beautiful fairy will smile and love again. You never gave me flowers. The meeting ends.

## Butterflowers

I learned it in school that thousands of moon years ago, butterflies fluttered from one flower to another in pursuit of sweet nectar. Over time, evolution combined butterflies and flowers into new creatures commonly known as butterflowers. These bloom beautifully in spring and summer.

I get out of work just in time to catch the warm rays of the setting sun cuddling butterflowers to sleep. Lazily they flap their wings, creating the circular aura of pollen about them. Excited spring bubbles rush to feed. How dare I be sad when such wonder surrounds me?

On my way to the Park, I pass the straight row of trees with blooming butterflowers raining pollen onto the expectant spring bubbles crowded below. Expectantly, I slow down when I reach the tree from under which a red bubble emerged yesterday. But nothing happens, and I stop to admire the tranquility of a newborn evening or to experience fully the first disappointment of the newborn evening not yet adulterated by my memories of you.

It occurs to me that I should take the matter into my own hands, and I put a lot of effort into breaking a big branch rich with green leaves and colorful butterflowers off the tree. I use it to lure some ten or fifteen spring bubbles to follow me to the Park.

Soon I reach the Meadow of Sorrow. Yours is not a blooming tree. There are no butterflowers or spring bubbles on the Meadow of Sorrow—that is why I wanted to bring a few on my own. I settle down, leaning against the trunk, and tease cheerful bubbles with my blooming branch. All they ever want is pollen. I close my eyes and remember.

## I Remember

I remember how we walked into The Village hand-in-hand, holding tight. The Village stands protected by mighty green woods. Butterflowers bloom there in all seasons, for all ages, for anyone who enters. No one ever has to leave and no one ever wants to, but sadly, everyone does. Each newly arrived couple gets a brand-new wooden house. The weather is always warm and so there is no need for indoor beds. Instead, the villagers sleep under the stars, on the roofs of their houses that are covered with soft grass and fragrant butterflowers.

You led the way into our house and I followed. I followed you onto the roof, my feet drowning in the cool, moist grass. I flapped my eyelashes to tickle your cheek. Your tongue licked across my cheek to my lips and we kissed nonstop, the heaviness of your body on mine making the kisses deeper than ever.

I took your hand and told you that it has ten fingers because the in-between fingers count too. I traced your in-between fingers with my tongue and then sucked the real ones. You fitted your real fingers into my in-betweens and our hands clasped into a lovers' fist. All night long you kissed my excited skin exposed to your skin, exposed to the boundless sky of countless stars.

In the morning our skin was marked with butterflower paint and pollen. I saw the blighted areas of the roof's green. I felt bad for the butterflowers we crushed with the heaviness of our bodies. I wanted to be consoled then, not left alone.

We dwelled in The Village for a period too brief. Afraid to

get me pregnant, unwilling to use condoms, perhaps bored of me, you walked away, leaving me in the ruined green to wait for you in the Meadow of Sorrow that could have been merry if only you came back.

## Shyknees

Thursday. Yesterday, before heading into the Park, I stopped by the store to buy the book over which Arby, the man with Rainbow Eyebrows, was so violently grimacing. I read it on my long way home and then in bed until sleepiness rendered the narrative senseless.

I find you in every character and blame the author's inefficiency for each detail that dares to deviate from what you would have done, said, or thought. I break the elements up and combine them in a way that would better fit you. I formulate my opinions about the book and speculate on how different would your review be from mine. My imagination is pure paradox. Your notions are so unique that upon hearing them I must take a few breaths before confusion transforms into awe. Your arguments are so surprising and unexpected that having an imaginary discussion with you is more than fiction. It is bad fiction. Bad fiction is less than fiction.

Noise from the arriving train gets my mind off fiction. As I enter the Quiet car, I am happy to notice Arby, on the same seat as yesterday, reading. But my eyes are captured by sunlight quietly playing on the knees of long, shapely legs in pantyhose. An attractive young woman about my age sits across from me. Her warmly shadow-painted eyes are closed, her head nods rhythmically to the music from her headphones. My eyes trace the pantyhose to the brim of a short black skirt and back to shiny knees—Shyknees. Shyknees has blond, blow-dried hair, French-manicured hands, and softly pink skin. Her face is no more beautiful than mine, but a complex union of shades and blushes creates profound shapes and shadows I could study for hours.

I allow myself to fancy Arby and Shyknees caught in a lovemaking act. Rhythmical nods of a young woman connected with a grimacing face of a handsome older man, both of them united by the mutual body motions forced on by the train.

The idea excites me to be brave. I get up to wait for my stop by the door, near Arby's seat, and interrupt his reading with a question of time. His face is displeased and distracted as he looks at his watch. But he raises his head and notices the book in my hands. The half-smile of recognition and vague interest bids me farewell as I get off the train.

## Tale of Talent Fairies

Hoping to avoid the misery, I avoid the Park. I go straight home after work, reading in the train, reading myself to sleep in bed. My dreams are always rich in colorful graphics. This night's dream is no exception.

Pieris Rapae, Eurema Lisa, Feniseca Tarquinius, Fixsenia Favonius were the ladies of the merry meadows of the green forest. It wasn't long until soldiers of the J army regiment, temporarily housed in these woods, discovered beautiful talent fairies. Each fairy had a single talent that was unknown to anyone, including herself. The first man to discover her talent became her master for life. Jack of the J regiment was first to capture a fairy. Libytheana Carinenta was short but shapely.

He found her naked by the roadside, feeding on butterflower nectar. The soldiers knew the tale of talent fairies and spent three days coming up with possible orders for Liby. John was hungry and ordered Liby to prepare dinner. Bound by magical powers, the fairy could not refuse. John became her master and Libytheana Carinenta became the J regiment cook. Each morning she left the camp for an hour, bringing back baskets of ripe fruits and berries. Wild birds and animals tamely followed behind her. Each day she prepared grand feasts of unmatched savor from the wild meat spiced with root juices and decorated with fresh green leaves.

Pieris Rapae was the next captive. Jeremy was the one to mouth the right order and the fairy became the weaver of clothes for the J regiment. No one knew from what plants or animals came threads so soft and colorful. No branches could tear the shirts Pieris Rapae made, no rain could pass through them, no dirt could stick to them. In the afternoon heat, her shirts cooled the soldiers' skin and warmed it from chilly evenings.

More and more talent fairies were brought into the camp, but Jack, the capturer of the first one, was still not a master of any. He spent months hunting through the forest until one day he came upon a tall tree. A fairy was kneeling beside it, all long legs and nakedness. Her hands clasped tightly around the trunk, her full breasts pressed firmly against it, her body pushed with energetic jerks against the tree. When Jack came closer, he noticed that her teeth were sunk into the bark and she sucked tree sap, which dripped all over her. The fairy paid no attention as Jack approached and he stood for a few moments wondering what to do next. The naked body continued pushing against the tree harder and harder. Jack took off his shirt and his pants and kneeled behind the fairy, his front demanding against her behind, his hands around her body sticky with tree sap, his lips vigorously sucking the sap off her neck.

Polygonia Comma followed Jack to camp. He did not explain Poly's talent to curious fellow soldiers but from the sounds coming from his tent that night, everyone knew and were jealous.

## Banished

Friday. I board the train and take a seat, comfortable in the space between Shyknees's legs and Arby's reading. The three of us belong together like a family. Arby raises his eyes and nods in recognition as I take the book out of my handbag. He does not look like a regular passenger on his way to work. Something about his manners and clothes makes me think of high-society saloons. I take a wild guess that he chose the Quiet train car as a morning escape where no one would bother him.

High-society train saloons are almost impossible to get into. They are for celebrities and millionaires. No one knows what happens there exactly, but the stories of nonstop parties always float around in the crowd. My friend has someone who belongs and promised to give me a one-ride pass for next week. I am very excited. Anything to get my mind off you.

I intend to read, but it is the end of the week and my eyes are closing all by themselves. I let myself drift into sleep and the dream continues.

Birds are chirping and butterflowers are blooming in the green, mighty woods. Everyone is jealous; every soldier in J army regiment wants to be a master of a talent fairy like Jack's. But Jack is not too excited anymore. His personality is complex; his desires are hard to satisfy. After a few months, he is bored of Poly. "I set you free, my darling lovely. Every man here worships you. You are free to go and choose any one you wish to stay with," he tells her, but the fairy only lowers her eyes and does not respond. Everyone wants her but cannot have her. She fights and bites, offering lovemaking only to her master. After weeks of following her indifferent Jack wherever he goes and refusing advances of every other soldier, crying Poly is driven out of the camp to restore everyone's peace of mind. Her misery is so great that she turns into a mermaid with green seaweed hair and a cold fish tail down from her waist. Several soldiers claim she tried to drown them when they sang songs by the pond after midnight.

I wake up because someone is tapping on my shoulder. "Pardon me, please, but I believe your stop is next," Arby tells me. Still full of my dream and confused by reality, I thank him and get off the train.

## Change

At the end of the day, I am able to avoid the Park again. I stand on the train platform and observe a well-dressed woman taking some change out of her pocket, considering it for a few moments, weighing the coins in her hand, and dropping them in the nearest garbage can. Why such an irrational action? Why? Why would she throw away a thing that gave her no trouble, a thing that might even be of benefit, however minor? Why did Jack banish Poly from his life? She was no burden to him, only pleasure. I don't understand.

I am in desperate need of change.

## My Laura

Saturday. I am in desperate need of change. I am also in desperate need to look my best before the next week's high-class saloon ride. Beauty saloon is just the place to visit. I arrive early and flip through the popular magazine while I wait in a comfortable armchair. My hands, my lap, my eyes, my thoughts fill up with glamorous wedding pictures. The young artist, the capturer of an ephemeral moon-heart image, married his girlfriend. As she declared her vows, the bride made a show of throwing out her old lucky coins and other charms because from that moment on, the only symbol of importance was her wedding ring. My heart squeezes in honest jealousy.

I tell the stylist I need a complete makeover. He implores me to be more specific but I can't, so he offers to open my Laura for a few days. Everybody has an aura that is filled with all the non-physical articles we carry with us. Activating my Laura will allow me to swim through my aura and decide what I do not like. The procedure is quite expensive, but I agree.

## My Aura

Sunday. I am Laura. I swim through the warm azure of sensation, through the air with fluid properties. I try to taste it but there is nothing to swallow, however hard I try. Precipitating lazurite crystals stick to my eyelashes, my brows, my hair. On contact with the skin, they dissolve into bluish vein-like streams distinct for some time against the lighter blue of azure substance.

There are shapes. Some hang motionless. Some fly past me,

carried by a current I cannot join, though it passes right by me. I am surrounded by yellow moons, spring bubbles, naked fairies, and other forms indistinct due to the clouds of pollen scattered by flapping wings of countless butterflowers. It tickles warm and fluffy. It is hard to see through the pollen powder, between the rotating moons and bubbles, beyond the beautiful fairy bodies. But I squint until it grows cold, until the blue turns to black and obstructions dissolve one by one, uncovering the heartbreak. Tears are streaming down my cheeks. I leave the aura, finding myself curled up on my bed, crying hard. If only I could have your hug now, if only just your hand on my shoulder, I wouldn't bite my lips for your kisses, I wouldn't look out the window feeling lonely and hopeless until I see a thousand moon spheres. I wouldn't make up fairy tales because I'd be living in one. There would be love, adventure, and marriage, and a happily-ever-after just like I was sure it would be when I was a child and read fairy-tale books with colorful pictures and magic narrative.

## Hawkbee

Monday. Waiting for the train to arrive, I spot a young woman in a black business suit of sharp-edge style: a bee-stinger body dressed in a black hawk beak. Hawkbee has a black hole for her aura. She sucks colors and forms from others. When the train arrives, I follow her into the Finance Morning car, curious. She smiles and rubs close by businessmen and women to absorb information and the general atmosphere of productive success. I guess she is getting ready for an important interview.

The welcoming host implores passengers to take their seats and offers coffee. The lecturer takes a sip from his cup, ready to begin. Two stops later when all seats are taken, the host introduces the lecturer as a professor famous for his research. I watch the stock market model that he prepared for today's discussion worm away from his aura into Hawkbee's. Disaster is inevitable. The professor should be starting his speech, but he is lost. I wish I could help, but there is nothing in my aura that could be of use to him now. Moments pass and the expectant silence gains tension. I pick up the newspaper and begin reading the front-page article, exporting the sentences over to the reddening speaker. He accepts, repeating the article word for word. Confusion, laughter hushed under propriety and respect, rolls through the audience. The lecturer edges his way to the door and runs out at the next stop, leaving the wide-eyed host to take over the podium.

## Nude

I exit Finance Morning into the adjacent A Painting a Day car. Many seats are empty because passengers prefer standing by the showcase. The painting under consideration is an enormous true-size reproduction of a modern piece titled "Untitled." The middle-aged woman host is suffering from an annoying audience member. The middle-aged man is so excited about color shades that he cannot help but interrupt her after each sentence to voice his insights. The blushing host is unable to resist. I move closer to the painting and sense much inside action expressing itself through colors.

I am Laura making my way through the warm azure. It isn't hard to swim from my aura into the excited man's. Mystic purple, raspberry red, vibrant violet. There aren't that many shapes in his aura, only colored fluids. Pretty pink, amber ale, ruby drunk heat. Two entwined bodies are lovemaking almost in public. His burgundy drips into her pink, her red lips on his brown hair. I am the neutral nude intruder, watching.

## Sneeze

I make it to the Quiet car. Arby raises his rainbow eyebrows quizzically. Did he worry over my absence? Does he expect me to be in my seat every day just as I expect of him?

Shyknees's eyes are closed. She is listening to her player as usual. So soft and inviting are her features that I wish this was a movie—a handsome man would get on the train and surprise her with a kiss. I sneak into my Laura and tiptoe to Shyknees's aura, careful not to wake her. Shock. Shock. Shock. Heavy beats of jarring, deafening music pulsate through the red and yellow gloom of her substance. I am stupefied. I cannot move away from all the hands, feet, breasts, torsos coming at me from all directions. Male and female, they touch me all over. Suffocating, scared, I cannot move. I cannot scream; I can only feel the flesh making me part of itself. I moan helplessly until the air current lifts me up and carries me to the outskirts of my aura. I swim into the depths of my azure, careful to seal all the entrances and prevent Shyknees's invaders from following.

Out of my Laura, I realize that the saving stream of air came from Arby's innocent sneeze accidentally directed at Shyknees. Their eyes meet: her eyes in search of the culprit who awakened her, his eyes apologetic, embarrassed by the violence of his sneeze. As for me, my infatuation with Shyknees is over.

## Azure Bubble

Aura-hopping makes me very tired by the evening. I go to sleep early, happy to be alone and safe in my bed.

In midsummer, butterflowers bloom most abundantly and flap their wings most intensely. Clouds of pollen mist hang over meadows. Spring bubbles feed until their membranes pop, sending fireworks of stored pollen into the air. Those that have a stronger, more elastic membrane grow into large, colorful spheres that wander through the woods until they burst.

Merry is the life of J army regiment. Jeffery is a master of Junonia Coenia, an extraordinary dancer. Jefferson enjoys Eurema Lisa, a gentle singer of sweetest lullabies. Every soldier has a talent fairy except for Jack. Jack does not need one; he is happy on his own. He could catch one easily but every time he comes across a fairy in the woods, he waits until the frightened, screaming beauty escapes. Only Poly never ran from him. She is gone now, and no one can match her.

Walking through the woods on a bright morning, Jack spots a youthful fairy playing with spring bubbles on the meadow, misty of pollen. So young and so fair, Jack has an urge to look away and preserve her undisturbed innocence. But the fairy sees him too. Instead of running away, she points a demanding finger at a big butterflower blooming on a nearby tree. No one tells Jack what to do, but this is most unusual. He climbs a tree and gets the butterflower. Cautiously, he approaches. The fairy's nakedness is sweet under sugary stains of colorful pollen, nectar, and paint from butterflower wings. Ceremoniously, she takes the big butterflower from Jack's hand, smiling like a child, looking into his eyes with playful authority. Something tender comes over them—a spring bubble of enormous size covers them from above and bursts into fireworks around them.

"I am Vanessa Virginiensis, and you are taking me with you," says the fairy.

No one tells Jack what to do, but this is most unusual.

"Why would you come with me?" he asks.

"Because I am bored of spring bubbles. I want to play with you," she answers.

Hand in hand, the couple walks into the camp. Jack takes care of his special fairy, but days pass and her talent remains a mystery. It is a major game between them. He wants to know her, but he can't. She wants to know herself, she wants to know him, she wants to know everything. She wants Jack to satisfy her whims, to get her beautiful butterflowers, to play with her all day long. No one tells Jack what to do, but this is most unusual.

Vanessa lived with Jack for a year before this special night. This night the youthful fairy is most playful. She tickles Jack's chest with a butterflower, not letting him fall asleep. She takes off the dress Jack always asks her to wear. She sits on his lap and whispers into his ear—"Tell me more about Poly." Maybe she is old enough, maybe her talent is the same as Poly's, thinks Jack, and hugs her closer. He is kissing her; he is licking butterflower nectar from her young, savory body. Vanessa is hot and quivering underneath. She is embarrassed to moan as Jack pushes in. She never played this game before and does not know the rules.

"What do I do, Jack, tell me, tell me what to do," she asks.

"Do what you want to do," he answers.

"I don't know what I want to do," she says, biting her lips and frowning.

In the morning, they do not speak much. Vanessa tries to bring back the cheer, but it is gone. She is not cheerful and neither is Jack.

"Go into the woods and find me an azure spring bubble," she orders. No one tells Jack what to do, and this is no longer unusual.

If only he brought that bubble... If only they tried again... If only he was able to guess her talent... "Love me"—was an order Vanessa never heard from Jack. If he discovered her talent, she could do anything. Her voice would never be as sweet as Eurema Lisa's, but her songs would please him the most. She would never cook as well as Libytheana Carinenta, but the food from her hands would be most tasty for Jack. She would not be as good as Poly, but he would forget Poly and be happy with Vanessa.

Jack never brings an azure spring bubble. He does not cast Vanessa away but refuses to play with her. Over and over she tries to bring back the old cheer but fails. Every day she goes to the meadow where they first met and sits there crying hard. As the moon years go by, her tears turn the meadow into the Meadow of Sorrow, drown it under the green pond. Burping frogs grow out of Vanessa's childlike beauty and her life becomes a continuous hunt for insects to ease her painful itching.

## Problems

Tuesday. I enter the Quiet train car and take my usual seat. Arby looks up from his reading and excitedly waves his new book in the air. I smile and nod and note the title. I wish I could tell you about this new game I've developed.

I left Arby's aura for last. My Laura is sore from past journeys. Slowly I approach his aura, hoping for cheerful welcome of healing rainbows. I think of the sun that smiles after a long series of rainy days and I walk ahead until my way is obstructed. Sheets of white paper make up the circumference of Arby's aura. They are math worksheets that his son needs help with. It did not occur to me that he could have children, a family. I consider turning back, but curiosity or desperation impels me to proceed. I read one of the problems—"Suppose there are four distinct tables with four people sitting around each table. How many ways are there to reseat the people so that no one is sitting with anyone they sat with before?" Discrete math was one of my favorite subjects. I look around for a writing device. Sure enough, there is a pencil floating nearby. I pick it up to work out the answer—$(4!)^4$. Glancing out of my Laura, I see Arby's eyes light up with solution. The worksheet page disappears, creating a gap through which I pass into his aura.

Book pages, many, many book pages, are still not enough to fill up his empty spaces. I float through the fluid of nothing and examine papers. I recognize a few to be the pages from the book we both read. There is a quarterly budget report for work. There is a recent divorce settlement. More math worksheets and tests his son failed. Great sadness emerges—for him, for me, for all whose dearest dreams proved to be an illusion, for all disappointed and all hurting.

I journey to my aura and back to Arby's, bringing him a bright butterflower. I know it would perish soon. Butterflowers are capricious creatures in need of constant attention and care. But let it bloom in his aura for as long as it may, flapping its wings and scattering rainbow colors of summertime cheer.

## Voicemail

My beauty saloon appointment is scheduled after work. I leave early to arrive on time. The stylist anticipates a long list of items to make over in my aura, but I decide to let it all be. My heartbreak hurts, but it is mine and not to be meddled with by a stranger's hands. He closes my Laura. I ask only for a haircut and highlights. They make me look fresh and happy.

At home I conduct a careful inspection of my frogs. Most of them dried up and fell off, leaving no trace, except in my memory. Hours pass while I select the right dress, matching shoes, luminous makeup. I haven't spent this much time by the mirror in moon years.

I think of the compliments I'll get tomorrow from my co-workers. I imagine how I will walk into the high-class saloon for my evening ride. I'd be going in a direction opposite from home, but convenience is not to be considered now. Convenience, you always care for convenience. Can it be that my growing attachment became inconvenient for you? I want to call you. I want to call you. I want to call you. I want to tell you about my exciting plans for tomorrow. I must not touch the phone.

It is time for bed. My outfit is ready. I am glamorous in the mirror. If I were you, I'd love me so hard. I'd kiss my long, beautiful hair. I'd look deep into the captivating green of my eyes. Tomorrow, I will not ask for autographs or photos. I am no less interesting or attractive than anyone I might meet there. I must not touch the phone. I do. My heart is beating loudly. I dial your number and listen to your away message. I hang up, leaving no voicemail. I left too many voicemails. It is time to sleep. Tomorrow will be good.

## Sunny Bunny

Wednesday. I have a spherical diamond pendant on my necklace and matching spherical earrings. The face of my hand watch is round too. It would make me very upset to have a rectangular-shaped watch. Oval is better but circle—the best.

The waterfall of morning sunlight bursts into the window of a sleepy Quiet train car. Bright rays kiss the sparkling face of my watch, opening the passage for a Sunny Bunny circle. It jumps from wall to wall, to a ceiling, onto the book Arby is reading.

It was you who captured Sunny Bunny when we lived in The Village. You followed it around our wooden house, you climbed furniture. My brave hunter, you pursued it when it escaped onto my body. On my thighs your hands tried to grasp it, on my stomach. Your lips covered Sunny Bunny on my breast. You held it in your mouth, smiling. I suggested we release it into the penthouse of my diamond watch. I promised to take good care of Sunny Bunny and let it out for occasional walks.

## Gems

I decided not to be nervous, but I am. I left work early to stand on the platform and wait. Two trains already passed. The next one is mine. I watch it approaching, just like any other regular train would. Second car from the head. I enter. A gorgeously made-up woman host with a smile too wide and too quick approaches me immediately.

"How are you today? May I see your pass, please?" she inquires, preparing to explain that this is a special car and I would have to please leave. I take the pass out of my handbag, embarrassed for no reason. The host takes it, looks at it carefully, and returns it with her big, fake smile. "Welcome. Please come in. Would you like me to get anything for you?"

I say no because I don't know what I could ask for. I was hoping she would introduce me to somebody, but she is already turning to walk away. What now?

Awkwardly, I walk between handsomely suited men and beautifully dressed women. They stand in circles talking, laughing, and drinking wine. They sit on the sofas in groups talking, laughing, and drinking wine. Some turn heads to look at me, a foreign passenger. A few faces are familiar, but I don't watch enough TV or read enough fashion magazines to know their names. I almost wish I was the excited, screaming fan interrupting everyone with, "Oh my! Are you really Jessica from Jessica Show? I love you! Can I have your autograph?"

Far into the saloon, I spot the fresh new wife of the moon-heart artist. She stands surrounded by a semi-circular crown of sparkling gem passengers. I walk over and blend into her crown. Next week, her husband and she are flying to a secluded tropical mansion for a honeymoon. They will be spending the whole summer there and their friends are all invited to visit.

"You'll be bored there after awhile, believe me," says a Red Gem.

Of course they would not. They will be taking weekends away from the tropics in Europe.

"Why don't you visit Rob and me in Venice," proposes a Silver Gem.

## Crown

I already accepted the fact that I will remain a silent Azure Gem for the entire evening, but someone puts a hand on my shoulder. I turn around. Arby. He looks so happy to see me.

"I never thought I can meet you like this," he says. "It's too bad Joe is not here today. He turns into such a recluse when working on his books."

"Joe?" I ask.

"Yes, the author of the book we both read. Did you finish it yet?"

"Yes, I have. A very even, transparent quillative. Like a dress on that Nude Gem to your right," I answer, lowering my voice so that Arby has to lean closer.

"You mean the pink dress?" he whispers back, surprising me, for I expected him to ask about quillative.

"Yes, but it's too nude for pink. I always visualize a novel as a glowing substance that contains its heart—its central message, perhaps the central image that inspired it. This substance is metaphysical, shapeless. The author has to materialize this substance by weaving a dress of narrative around it: a quillative. Quality quillative has to be even without any knots or holes, but it is not enough. Most importantly, it must be transparent, allowing readers to look deep into the enclosed substance and feel its presence, its intangible complexity."

"Shapeless? I must disagree about shapeless, at least as far as Nude Gem is concerned!" says Arby, disappointing me even more.

"Nude Gem is not metaphysical either. If we map her dress to a quillative, her body must be mapped to an idea, which is shapeless."

"I wish Joe was here to argue this one. What do you think of the sudden change he made in the middle?"

"I think he took off from the Eiffel Tower and landed in a Vegas casino."

Arby's rainbow eyebrows ask for explanation.

"As I picture it, in the beginning of most books I am an archeologist exploring the pyramids of Egypt. New characters, new settings. I don't know what treasures or horrors await me in the next room—mummies, gems, spider webs. There are grand halls, narrow corridors, secret passages. Once the introduction is fully completed, I begin climbing the well-defined structure of the Eiffel Tower. New action logically flows from the previous, heading into the sky until the story exhausts itself into the final zenith syllable.

"But in our book, the author jumped off the middle of the Eiffel Tower and landed in Vegas, next to the winning slot machine. I was irritated at first but his ending left me exuberant with clinking clapping of jackpot."

I look around and realize that a crown of gems gathered around Arby and me. He crowned me! He offers me wine. Conversation shifts to life abroad. I am silent now because I had never actually been to Egypt or France, England or Switzerland, but I remain the accepted queen of my circle.

Gradually the circle breaks up as passengers get off the train on their stops. Arby offers more wine. He does not care for my other opinions on literature and does not express his own. He tells me about his twelve-room apartment with the Park view. He invites me over.

## Descent

The street is dark and quiet when we get off the train.

"It's only two blocks away," Arby tells me, and I follow. We pass the row of sickly trees with decaying butterflowers that flap their chipping wings.

Doorman. Elevator. Keys. He turns the light on but it is still cold.

"Wow, antique furniture."

"I got divorced a year ago."

"I know."

I see relief in Arby's eyes. He wants someone who knows, who accepts, who will make it all good again.

"Hold on a second. You're going to love this. Just one second," he says and leaves the room.

Reality overwhelms me. I wanted to see the apartment, not stay here. I cannot do it. Not outside The Village.

I look out the window at a dark sky full of moons. Fire escape. Escape. I open the window and climb out onto the narrow steps. A thought of letting go into the abyss is unavoidable, but my hands hold on tight as if my body decided to take over and control my being until I reach safety. Forty-eight, forty-four, forty, thirty-six, thirty-two, twenty-eight, twenty-four, twenty, sixteen, twelve, eight, four, one. Arby appears at the window when I reach the first floor.

"Come back here, my crazy girl." He is holding an enormously sized book.

Even though I cannot see his eyes, I believe they glisten with anguish. I can feel his hands tightening around the book that he extricated from the shelf so excitedly just a moment ago. I want to make it all good for him, but I cannot. I will never find out what's in his giant book.

"Stay there, I will be right down," he yells.

I jump, landing on my hands and knees. They do not hurt just yet. I run down the empty streets for a long time.

**Peace**

Thursday. Friday. I take two days off work to stay in bed with sunflower seeds watching TV. Each mawkish scene of sentimental music and earnest revelation makes my eyes teary. I am surprised at this new level of sensitivity I was never burdened by until now. Dull pain reminds me of bloody, bandaged knees under the covers. I am so proud of them.

Fitness club, beauty saloon, designer dresses, expensive jewelry, dance lessons. I make the list of things that are worthless without you. England, France, Italy, Egypt, Prague vacation plans, graduate school, high-class saloon parties, gems, and crowns. More things. I will have them all, because it's the best course of action. I did look up to you as to a man I can discover the world with. I lost you but still have the world, many worlds to explore on my own. Expect to receive regular reports of my lonely journeys. I will not call or e-mail. Spring bubbles will bring you my messages, kisses, and butterflowers.

Water that could spill out of the boiling pot already did. The fire is out now and my burning tempest calms into acceptance.

## Trap

Saturday. Morning sunlight streams through the window and ignites my hand watch with sparkles. Sunny Bunny is out of the trap that we created for it in The Village. I try to release it completely, but it wouldn't go. Sunny Bunny made a home in my circle penthouse watch. I look at the time for comfort.

MICHAEL CHEVAL 2007

# Loverfly

I WAS YOUNG THEN AND MADE my first web—very crooked and useless indeed— between two apple trees. Catching flies is not an easy task, and I went hungry for days, watching as my more successful brothers and sisters competed against each other in number and size of trapped insects. I was about to lose all hope when the wind brought me a dandelion seed on a white, web-like parachute that got entangled in the strings of my home. How scared and excited I was all at the same time! I hid in the bark's fold and could not stop my second right leg from twitching. When web vibrations stopped, I climbed out to examine the prey. Bitter was my disappointment when I discovered my catch was nothing but a dandelion seed on a white parachute. How the neighboring spiders made fun of me then!

Days passed. I looked and looked at the parachute, considering its symmetrical, thin strings until I made up my mind to rebuild my web. A larger, more transparent house caught me the first two flies. Soon I was good friends with the parachute, but it was not enough. I wanted to amaze him, to dazzle him. I was falling in love with my Loverfly.

While my sisters were busy finding husbands and settling their homes, I was rebuilding mine over and over, experimenting with different web-designs to amuse Loverfly. Deeply involved in my art, I paid no attention to hunting. Neighbors—who liked to look at my web-designs as well—saved me from hungry death on numerous occasions. They kept telling me that my romance with Loverfly was fruitless, but what did I care for food or husbands or conventions! Loverfly and I were happy together until our problems began. He felt that stuck in my web, he was not living his life to a full potential. We had many arguments until I could let my Loverfly go. Down to the ground he went, and that day my house was adorned with little crystals of spider tears.

Everyone now expected me to begin a normal spider life, but I was too sad. Working on my web reminded me of Loverfly and our life together, so I abandoned it. Most days I spent hidden in the folds of the apple tree bark. Compassionate neighbors gave me some of their fly remains to keep me alive.

Days passed. One morning—driven out of the bark by hunger—I saw my dear Loverfly in the form of a yellow dandelion flower, right below my web. Our happiness was back. He grew higher toward me and I rebuilt my web close to his golden hair. All the world was wrong about us—our romance was a miracle, we made it in our own unique way. These were wonderful times of love and splendor. Gorgeous Loverfly attracted hundreds of flies and beautiful, fat butterflies. Some of them we let go, others I caught for food, many of them I presented to neighbors to repay and greatly overpay my debts.

Every morning I climbed onto my Loverfly and looked up into

the eternity of sky blue. I embraced the universe—me, a little gray dot hugging yellow petals—I embraced the grand, the amazing, the incomprehensible—how I kissed those yellow petals!

Our happiness lasted long. Most of my sisters had little spider kids by this time. But Loverfly's golden hair began turning white—more and more so each day—inevitably and natural. His once tender petals were now dry. I watched as the wind scattered our love and hoped it would bloom again in other parts of the world. I looked and looked until there was nothing else to see. And here I am.

MICHAEL CHEVAL 2007

# *The Cell of a Soul*

STRAIGHT COLUMNS LINED UP NEXT TO each other and strict rows lying under one another form an unbroken grid of cells ruled by unbreakable borders. Of course, some of the borders can be changed by merging the cells together, but this would happen under a special circumstance dictated by certain application needs and would not damage present order.

Imagine yourself stuck between Excel cells—pale cells, colorless. What if you were also pale and colorless all throughout—all throughout but for the single cell of your soul. Since its birth, L9 could feel the commotion, some unsettling urge, but none of that reflected onto its visible surface. For a while it wondered what color is that cell of its soul and began to look around for an answer. A few faraway cells were blue, one was green, and C8:E8, D9:D18, C20:E20 were red. How bright were those red cells! Their flaming, screaming color pierced L9's eyes and illuminated its soul, making the strange cell of its soul visible—it was red.

Now no matter where L9 looked, it had a light. The red color spread from one cell of its soul to others, creating more and more commotion and desire. L9 dreamed about being marked with red color and of taking the place of D19, where it would enjoy the light of its neighbors and illuminate them in return with the same intensity. How unpleasant it was to return from a fantasy and find oneself surrounded by colorless cells that now appeared to L9 paler than before. It was even more unpleasant to understand the impossibility of moving through the borders. But the most unpleasant was the realization of one's own colorlessness.

L9 brooded, finding itself glowing at one moment and dimmed the next. It would probably continue on in this state, but sudden changes forced it to pay more attention to its neighbors. L8 became merged with L7, and K9 was colored in yellow, although the others talked of the color as gold. L9 held its breath, hoping that some changes might be applied to it as well, but nothing happened. How could that be? Why was it so unlucky? L9 wondered then whether the neighboring cells felt something similar to its own turmoil and decided to ask.

M9 had especially solid borders and looked more upright and true than many others. L9 turned to it for guidance, hoping to steady its own wavering soul. M9's opinion was that every cell was put in its place for a purpose, and its duty to the law of application is to proudly bear whatever contents are written in it and whatever color it is marked with. Thus, it is shameful to ever think of being red if you are not marked so for the reasons beyond control or understanding. The border between M9 and L9 grew even thicker, although this could not be distinguished by someone looking at the computer screen. L9 was surprised by such harsh opinion, but knowing no other, it thought it might be right. From now on it tried not to imagine itself on the place of D19, but since that did not calm the cells of its soul, L9 decided to look for another opinion.

L10 had much thinner and paler borders, and L9 thought it might be safe to address this sickly cell. L10 was surprised to hear of L9's fantasies. It looked as if it had trouble coming to terms with the shocking novelty of L9's words. How could somebody think of such a thing—to become red and to relocate! Yes, it does sound quite interesting, but there is no point to think of that, which is not possible. It is so much better not to dream of something that can never be. L9 now felt itself a hopeless dreamer. It convinced itself again and again that its dreams could never come true. But logic and dreams exist independently of each other, and so from now on, L9 told itself that it can never be red every time before imagining itself red. Thus, not finding guidance or council, L9 continued the inquiries.

The borders of L8 were paler at certain points and brighter at others, creating a wavy appearance. Sensual curves looked like momentary shivers caused by accidental touch. Since L8 was now merged with L7, it was among the biggest cells in the application, and L9 concluded it might have some good advice. L8 was happy and did not want to talk of anything but its happiness, but after prolonged inquiries it disclosed its secret. There was a time when it also wished to relocate. It happened when it became united with L7. How strange it felt to share one's life with an alien cell. How scary it was to be exposed after the border was removed. But then it found out that L7 was scared too, and also wished to relocate. They soon discovered how similar they were in what they felt and what they wanted. Two cells—true soul mates. Maybe all L9 needed to do was to find its soul mate. L9 considered this advice. Since its direct neighbors did not seem interested, L9 looked at K8, M8, K10, and M10 respectively. Although it was able to recognize some of their distinctive features, they were too far apart to understand one another.

The only cell that L9 did not talk to was K9, the golden cell. The inner walls of its borders were illuminated by its yellow color. Carefully, L9 formed its inquiries for the fourth time. K9 never wished for any particular color or location, but always wanted to be distinguished among others, and apparently became known to the neighborhood as a special cell even before it was marked as such. Maybe if L9 waited long enough it would be colored yellow too, since very often neighboring cells are similarly marked. For the present, L9 was welcome to enjoy the gold emitted from this important neighbor.

After this conversation, L9 really did feel distinguished and honored to be close to K9. They often talked to each other, and L9 was ready to agree with everything K9 said. Slowly the cells of L9's soul illuminated by the special neighbor began, under the effect of golden light, to appear yellow. Eventually the soul of L9 became as good as yellow, except for one cell. As the golden light touched this one cell with its yellow rays, L9 felt its usual burning passion with such strong force as never before, and its gaze turned away from K9 to the red cells. Momentarily, L9's soul again became red, brighter than before. All around, L9 now saw colored cells. They were green, blue, red, yellow, or white. Their borders were bright, pale, solid, thin, thick, straight, wavy, and of many other countless forms and combinations. Looking at them, L9 felt that it was the only cell lacking its true color. Desperate, lost, but hopeful, it began forming words of prayer that became visible within its borders.

Now if you are working late in the evening and suddenly see words appear in one of the Excel cells, you know what you must do. Read the words. Ctrl-X and Ctrl-V L9 cell into D19 position, previously, of course, saving D19 on the clipboard so it can be put in place of L9. Then you color D19, which in reality is L9, with red. Having done so, you realize that it is time to stop what you are doing and get on your way. But before saving and closing the application, it is worthwhile to notice how bright the L9 cell is in its true home among the neighbors that are now made brighter by it. Report would never become completed otherwise.

MICHAEL CHEVAL 2007

# *Autumn Symphony*

Early in the chilly New York morning, he entered her. Suddenly awake and startled, as she was at the beginning of each new day, she growled a disapproval, which gradually softened into a cat's purr, for she did not realize until now how cold she was, almost frozen, and how warm he felt inside her, spreading the waves of heat and energy throughout her body until she was fully awake and ready to ride. She loved this time of morning tenderness when, yawning, he settled into her lap, caressed her wheel with his warm hands, sometimes whispered under his breath, "Come on, baby. That's my girl."

Streets were still dark around them. He turned on the radio, a classical station as usual. She never knew much about classical music before he became her driver. He wasn't her first, but the first one who mattered. She enjoyed his confidence, the sure way in which he handled her, both soft and rough at the same time, his touch never forceful but never insignificant.

She never had a chance to look into his eyes yet, though surely someday the circumstances will let that happen—he will put her on emergency brake and walk out in front of her headlights while the engine is still running. Then she will focus on his eyes, and everything within her frame of vision will become painted with his eye color, which she will treasure forever in her memory. That's how car vision works—they see in black and white until they focus on a particular object, and everything becomes dyed with the object's color. By design, cars are meant to focus on traffic lights and immediately recognize their colors without being distracted by surrounding ones. If everything is green, it is safe to proceed; if red, it is best to stop. Cars try to pass their awareness on to their drivers, whose subconscious senses can sometimes respond to these signals, although it does not work consistently all the time.

Cars have the ability to learn new signals and meanings. Seeing an unusual traffic light color, the car can observe her driver's actions and apply her knowledge next time. She was eager to absorb new discoveries just like any other car, only the things she usually learned were not only useless for her intended functionality but distracted her from simplest responsibilities.

The two most important things she learned from her present driver were the pleasure of classical music and the ability of accompanying each chord with an appropriate color. There were yellow sounds, red, blue, gray, as many sounds as there are colors. She used up terabytes of memory mapping and remapping sounds to colors to objects, focusing on which produced the desired color. Hearing sentimental notes, she consulted her map for yellow and focused her eyes on China roses sold on the sidewalk. Gray warnings combined with pavement, with pigeons. Red fortissimo drowned with the intensity of the setting sun. All summer long, she played with tints of rich green, but as the autumn approached, all previous mappings were as good as useless. Now she was inundated by the variety of expression found among autumn leaves. She learned to recognize the types of trees, and which ones were likely to have yellow leaves, as opposed to red or brownish. Lately, however, she began abandoning her map altogether in order to focus on random leaves and have them paint the music. Whatever streets, directions, and road signals she ever knew about were long lost. Her driver was left to figure them out on his own, but she knew she could trust him. He would always lead the way and drive safely, always knowing where to go and how to get there.

Biting chilliness of the morning striped the intruders who entered its dark kingdom of the warm tokens they tried to hide in the folds of their clothing and gradually receded with retreating darkness, unable to escape its defeated home of shadows. She was victorious riding into the new day, her bright yellow outfit sparkling down the streets. Tchaikovsky's Fifth Symphony streamed from her radio, and she played in its waves, swimming and diving in the color pools that splashed the road, the buildings, the sky with autumn leaf colors. Suddenly, and for her it was usually sudden, she had to stop. Hesitant hands opened her door, and sharp heels dug into her skin as a young woman entered.

"Could you turn up the volume, please?" the woman said, her voice matching her hands in its shy uncertainty.

Why must there always be strangers entering into their privacy? Her driver was the only one who made her regret being a taxi. Taxis are proud of their independence, their continuous adventures, their thick anthologies of collected conversations and personalities. But how gladly would she give it all up to be a private car belonging to her driver, to know that she was the one chosen out of all others, to be cared for, be fixed and loved instead of used by a continuous stream of strangers.

"Of course I can. You like classical music?" The driver turned to look at the young woman.

"Love it. Columbia, please. 116th and Broadway," she replied.

This was unusual. No passenger ever mentioned the barely audible music. The Fifth Symphony was Taxi's favorite, and it hurt to share it with a stranger. She felt as if the young woman's heels were piercing her heart.

"You taking classes there?" continued the driver.

"Yes, grad school," the woman said, looking out the window. "Such a beautiful day outside, it's a shame to be stuck indoors all day."

"What are you studying for?"

"High school English teacher."

Some teacher she was if every statement she made sounded like a vague question. Personal shyness aside, the source of her pronounced nervousness might be the driver. A handsome man, whose playful tone made him irresistible, he often obliged female passengers to sit with their backs straight and their gestures unnatural. He was a very interesting man, striking all sorts of sophisticated discussions if the passengers were inclined to participate. He talked politics, arts and literature, history. He flirted easily with pretty women, getting their wide smiles and phone numbers that he stuck in his pockets. Taxi learned from his thoughts that he used to be a history professor at some university. There was something about a Shakespeare club with his students, about being over thirty-five and single, grading essays, a decision to leave his job and become a taxi driver in order to prove some point only a few devoted students were smart enough to understand.

"Really? An English teacher, huh? Why would you willingly commit yourself to such misfortune?" The driver turned to face the young woman and smiled. "Joking, of course. I am a history professor on a break. Will be resuming my responsibilities in a couple of months."

Really? He will leave so soon? Really? He told the truth about himself? Her driver never disclosed his former occupation or identity when he flirted. What wild stories he came up with about his life to amuse wide-eyed girls who chose to believe every word he chose to utter!

"How soon can you get out of classes?" the driver asked, having considered "can" as opposed to "will."

"Well, I have to go to this first one, but I am thinking to cut the rest. It is too beautiful a day. So I'll be free in two hours."

"Would you care for a taxi waiting for you right here on this corner?" Taxi found herself stopping by the sidewalk, one block away from Columbia campus.

“Yes, I’d like that.” The woman wanted to add something else but fell silent instead.

“There’s a symphony orchestra playing in Central Park today. One of those concerts-in-the-park events. We could drive by there. If you are cutting classes, I have to cut work, just to be even.”

“I’ll see you in two hours,” said the woman, smiling brightly. She opened the door and stepped out. Taxi was happy to be rid of those sharp heels.

They drove a reticent young man downtown to the South Ferry and picked up an inconspicuous middle-aged woman heading to the Union Square area. Taxi and her driver were too involved in their own thoughts to pay these transitory guests any attention. Taxi read and reread the words from her voice-cache memory registry: “There’s a symphony orchestra playing in Central Park today.” She copied the message into her main memory and continued moving it from one memory address to another, duplicating it and resaving it, unable to cope with the excitement of its meaning. The grand, the impossible dream Taxi cherished ever since she fell in love with the music was to hear the real, the true live orchestra. The only grander and more impossible dream was to be a private car belonging to her driver. If only he felt like she felt. What a day this could be if he took her to that concert! Imagine making detours through Central Park between every passenger ride. And why not? Were they not an ideal team, always doing their job? What joy, what a grand majestic experience to be led by her driver down the autumn alley toward a yellow-red meadow with musicians and their instruments. What color were they, the instruments? No, she would probably not find out; it would be far too important to focus on the lavish selection of autumn colors to match the intensity of live music.

Taxi gathered up her full resources, trying to communicate her desires to her driver. But this was a problem from the start of their relationship. No messages she ever sent reached his thoughts, and she gave up altogether, satisfying herself with the delight of simply existing by his side, with the pleasure of having him inside her. But this time it was important, it was imperative that he heard her.

Heading uptown along Broadway, they fell into a heavy traffic. A gleaming-white limo, carrying a wedding party, was conversing with a big, dusty truck and a miniature private car.

"I take them on the first ride of their marriage," declared the snow-bride limo, "and I am responsible for constructing a backbone for their relationship, a railway of values to keep them on track as they continue their journey. I am concerned about trust, stability, and safety. They have fun along the way, but all fun ends as soon as these values are compromised. No one wants to get a police ticket or much worse, be involved in a crash. That's why I devoted myself to safety algorithms. For instance, what's the basic rule for a red light? Two meters before the crossing, you focus on traffic light color, and tell your driver to stop or to go. I do not think this is nearly enough. I came up with my own formulas. As soon as we enter the street, I start looking for the traffic light. There are some approximate values I acquired over the years by timing the duration of yellow, red, and green in various locations. So midway down the street, I can determine if the traffic light would change when we near it, and I can start preparing my driver for appropriate actions."

"That is all very interesting, but these kinds of calculations are of little concern for my functionality," replied the giant, heavy truck. "I rarely have to drive through big cities. Highways are my domain. I have to travel across states to deliver my inventory, and hence, have to worry about memory management. Imagine having to store all the names and exit numbers. My driver, he is good, but without me, we would have gotten off track so many times. Keeping a one-to-one mapping of destinations to direction sequences is impossible. Instead, I keep all the names and numbers in a Locations array. Then, for each destination, I store a string of indexes into the Locations array, in the appropriate order. Once I am on the road, I parse the string back into indexes and look up the sequence of directions. It gets much more involved than that, of course, when I need to cross-reference the strings to determine the best path if, say, a highway was closed, and we had to take an alternate route. My driver is always surprised how he manages to make right decisions. He calls it 'intuition.'"

"Girls, all this will be useless unless you figure out a way of establishing a reliable connection with your driver," pronounced a silver private car. "There are two ways of handling communication: the power of suggestion, and the more reliable direct connection. To use the power of suggestion, you could send the same message continuously over a few minutes, hoping that at least one makes it to your driver's thoughts. It works better if you synchronize with his breathing and forward only when he exhales. His body is usually more relaxed then, and his mind more receptive. I, however, prefer a reliable direct connection. It takes awhile to establish, but then you can send your message and read his thoughts for verification of successful receipt. It took much practice, but we managed. We spend lots of quality time together."

None of the cars even mentioned the concert, and yet instead of swelling with the usual contempt for their ignorance, Taxi felt a pinch of anguish, as if the young woman's sharp heels were once again piercing her from within. All these cars accomplished something so basic, so ordinary and essential that it was incomprehensible how Taxi managed to avoid doing this altogether. All these cars offered something to their drivers and passengers. And what did she, Taxi, offer? Nothing. She was nothing to her driver but a shell he used for the everyday necessity of driving. She was replaceable; she was useless.

Traffic dissolved, and they turned off Broadway, continuing their way uptown. Desperately Taxi listened to her driver's breaths and sent him messages. She tried to concentrate and establish a reliable connection, but all was in vain. All right then, not everything was lost; she would still get to attend the concert, even if she had to tolerate the presence of that student-teacher girl.

What if he tried to kiss the girl … inside her? She felt it before she knew it, and she knew it before she heard it—the familiar sounds of Tchaikovsky's Fifth Symphony streamed from somewhere within the park. If they go on to pick the young woman up, the symphony will be over, over completely, over forever. The driver placed his foot on the brake, but it fell through, and they sped over the crosswalk on the red light. Technology was not working, familiar mechanisms failed—Taxi followed the music into the park. Down the glamorous autumn alley glimmered the yellow Taxi, proudly carrying her terrified driver. Kissed by the bright afternoon sun, she almost ignored his fists hitting her wheel. She focused on leaves with hundreds of variations in their tints, their tones, their meanings, and feelings. Through her eyes, one fascinating color replaced the other painting the world. The symphony blinked with saturated yellow of deep yearning and vibrant red of ultimate victory. So greatly Taxi wanted to share her vision with the driver that she began flooding him with a stream of color messages.

Panic stripped his mind of secure firewalls of reality that allowed only the graspable, the comprehensible to pass through and preserve the safe comfort of his being. Suddenly receptive to anything directed his way, the driver lost his sight of surroundings as colors blinked before his eyes. Colors blinked and the music grew louder. Rushed by the excitement of the music, by the unexpected success at getting through to her driver, Taxi wanted to impress him by sharing everything bright and precious that was stored in her registers. She sent it all out at once, forgetting to save backups for herself. When the intensity of the moment reached beyond the bearable limit, both the Taxi and her driver became suspended in the infinity of sound and color, deafening and blinding. It passed when the music grew silent.

* * *

The symphony does not end with the triumph of its last chord. It continues into the silence, into the reaction of its audience. It ends only when we forsake it in our minds to focus on other thoughts. Anxiously, Taxi waited through the silence for her driver's reaction. Her empty registers felt uncomfortably exposed and sensitive. Her wheel hurt.

The driver's response came promptly as he regained control and drove out of the park. They were heading downtown now, to the cab base. Could he not forgive her this once? She tried sending a message but failed. If only she could communicate with him again, Taxi would tell him that she meant no harm, that she got carried away, that she was so very sorry for risking his and her own well-being. Couldn't they turn around and go to Columbia to pick up the girl? She was probably still standing there, waiting. Couldn't they bring everything back the way it was? No, sooner or later it was bound to happen. She did have something to offer, but the great gift she offered was not acceptable for her driver. He was an amazing man of exceptional intelligence, but the threads of his logic, the beliefs hardwired into his mind, did not allow him to receive her messages, to understand her, or even to perceive her existence, the possibility of her and of her world. He was shocked; he was terrified; his response expressed his reaction toward the physical situation of a broken car. The symphony of sound and color he altogether ignored, proving his inability of perception and denial of participation.

Taxi knew what was to happen next. He will take her to the base and leave. After awhile she will be examined by mechanics, their rough hands searching through her privacy. Eventually, having found nothing physically wrong with her, they will assign Taxi to a new driver.

It all happened so suddenly. If only she had more time to practice communication. If only she had learned to share her driver, to accept the taxi status of their relationship, and be his ally in risky girl adventures. No, she could not be satisfied with half-happiness. Half-happiness was not happiness, no matter how many times Taxi replicated and saved her part of their relationship within her registers. Her love was a right-hand piano melody played without the left-hand part. She was a symphony played out without him listening.

Hopefully, this frightful experience will convince her driver to leave his job and resume his professorship. She'd like that much better than to think of him in another taxi. Driving by universities, she will now imagine him somewhere out there, listening to classical music. Another New York heart broken. No more love to drive her, no more music, no more colors—I close my eyes, I close my eyes now.

# Childhood Story Revised

RED LAY ON HIS BACK, LOOKING up at the sun and smiling. He was just like all other fallen leaves that colored the ground with autumn paint, except for big, surprised eyes and a wide smile, pen-drawn across his red surface. Red knew that summer was over, but he greeted every phase of leaf-life with joyful curiosity, eager to experience new adventure as it came. He had welcomed the quiet snap that separated him from a tree and the gentle wind that danced with him all the way to the ground. Then he was lifted up on a small palm. A child took a pen out of its pocket and blessed Red with big eyes and a wide smile, capturing so precisely the leaf's character. Red marveled at the gift, wishing the adventure would continue, but the child dropped him back to the ground and ran off.

For three days, Red lay on his back, smiling at the sun, and waiting for something to happen next. An alarming thought slowly crept through his amber veins that no longer transported nutrition throughout his body—"It is all over. It is all over for me."

"Oh, you bet it is," echoed Brown, a shriveled, gloomy leaf who had been on the ground for a much longer time.

"Speak for yourself," replied Yellow, "I have many plans for settling my future. I am sure some young girl will pick me up and store me in her diary. Judging from my appearance, I am very well-suited for this purpose." Yellow adjusted her position, pushing aside the newly fallen leaves to remain visible on the surface.

"Stop smiling, Red. Accept the end with dignity and understanding, not the smile of an ignorant clown," urged Brown.

"Yeah, Red, stop smiling. You were not gifted. You were marked, marred, dirtied. No one will pick you up now," pronounced Yellow, her yellow cheeks blushing lightly with rosy spots.

Red's big, surprised eyes now filled with sadness. He tried to curl up, to force on wrinkles and hide his smile in them. How tragic it is to grow brown and crumble into nonexistence. Every leaf—a poem, a story with words and worlds in their colors. Another Universe grows them like a tree, and they leave it at the end of summer with a quiet snap of a pen or a keyboard. Down they fall onto the paper, hoping to continue their journey in diaries, libraries, and memories. But so few of them make it in their afterlife.

So it was revealed to me when I found Red, with big, surprised eyes and a wide smile, pen-drawn across his red surface by a small child playing in the park. Or was it a story written in childhood that I found among paper leaves crumbled under a wooden plank in the attic, which used to be a secret place where I hid things? I noticed Red, I picked him up from the ground, smoothed his wrinkles, revising him, allowing his wide smile to shine, his big eyes to fill with surprise and wonder.

MICHAEL CHEVAL 2007

# *Lying and Lovely Left*

**SCENE 1**

*Two bars are constructed on the stage—one just above the floor, another higher. Two women in identical dresses of slightly different tones of beige stand on the lower bar with their hands holding on to a higher bar.*

*When the curtain opens, both women are found next to each other with their heads and arms lowered, possibly hanging over the higher bar—as the two stockings would be hanging on the rope after being washed. When they begin talking, they can start moving as the length and construction of the bars permit, but until the end of the scene, neither can step down to the floor.*

*Lighting is dim, amber, mysterious.*

Dreamy Right: I feel like hanging myself.

*(Now louder and with more desperation.)*

I feel like hanging myself!

Wise Right: I think you are repeating it for the hundredth time. Why, just why was I paired up with such thoughtlessness, such weakness. Either you are in a blissful flight through the skies of unreasonable happiness or you are in the darkest depths of inconsolable desperation.

Dreamy Right: And I am tired of your continuous, endless, detached, devoid of all feeling analysis of everyone and everything. And you are not happy either. I am desperate; you are depressed. I don't see one being better than another.

Wise Right: You are so underdeveloped. If only I could teach you anything. But no, all my efforts are wasted. You cannot be improved.

Dreamy Right: I can't stand the likes of you. You are someone who can sit down to learn a foreign language but cannot sit back to simply enjoy the sounds of unknown words.

Wise Right: Yes, I believe learning a language would be much more reasonable than wasting time dreaming away, listening to sounds. If I was fated to get the second Left in my life, why should she be so, so … so wrong?

Dreamy Right: You are wrong. I am no Left pair of yours. I am Right, as much Right as you are, only newer and better.

Wise Right: I am older and hence wiser. You must accept that.

Dreamy Right: You are older and hence less new.

*(Pause)*

You are older and hence less desirable.

*(Pause)*

No wonder I don't get to dance so much. Oh, the time when I was with my left pair-mate, my dear Lovely Left! Those were the days! Sometimes we danced the whole night away. Hardly sat down. All you want to do is hide underneath the chair and judge everyone. These socks are low-class, these are middle-class, these are high-class but messy, which makes them smellier than good middle-class. Who thinks about that! And when yesterday we finally got onto the dance floor, you were totally lost.

Wise Right: I have a small stitch. You cannot see it when I am worn. I am careful not to get ripped again.

Dreamy Right: Right, you are afraid. That's why you always criticize me. You are jealous because I am not afraid to dance, to dream.

Wise Right: Not afraid to dream but unable to think is a dangerous combination. You really think I am jealous of you? That must be some pleasant feeling that you grow in the comfortable hours of warm sweat in your shoe. I consider you in all respects inferior to myself. You've only been worn to parties that I've been lowered to after losing my left pair-mate, my Lying Left. You haven't seen anything but the twilight of bars and clubs. No one ever sees you there. Now in my days, I have been worn to offices with fancy shoes and classic suits. I have been to conferences in London, Tokyo, New York. I maintained the most proper etiquette and was in a perfect fit with the other handbags, socks, ties, gloves, handkerchiefs that filled the brightly lit corporate rooms and were all noticed and judged. There I sat with my back straight—correct, classic, gorgeous.

Dreamy Right: Conferences? So tell me about your life. If telling stories is not too beneath you.

Wise Right: What's the point? You won't hear half of it with your lack of concentration and won't understand the other half with your lack of thinking.

*(Pause)*

Okay, I will tell.

*Lights dim to black. Bars are carried off the stage.*

**END OF SCENE**

## SCENE 2

*Brightly lit stage. A woman in a wide costume sits on the floor—a handbag. Right in front of her is a man, partially covered with her costume—a wallet in a handbag. Grey cardboard walls with oval airplane windows might be placed on the sides of the stage. Wise Right and Lying Left stock-walk onto the stage—that is, one walks ahead of the other, stops, waits for the other to get in front, then walks ahead again, thus resembling stockings moving with the feet. As soon as they sit down on the floor, the standard airplane greeting sounds, first in English and then in French.*

<u>Wise Right</u>: Learning French would be a nice memory exercise. My Lying Left, what do you say we start when we get back home from this trip.

<u>Lying Left</u>: Yes, Wise Right, knowing more languages is always advantageous. French might come in handy in the future.

*(Pause)*

How I like these trips abroad, and how I hate the airplanes.

<u>Wise Right</u>: I don't see why you would be afraid. You won't suffer too much in case of a crash. Just mere seconds …

<u>Lying Left</u>: Shut up, shut up, shut up. Who said anything about a plane crash? You can't talk about a crash in the plane.

*The plane is about to take off. The engine roar is heard.*

Lying Left: Ohhh, this is the worst moment—the take off.

*Wise Right patronizingly extends her hand to hug Lying Left. Lying Left hides her face on the shoulder of Wise Right and the airplane take-off sound is heard. After some time, Lying Left raises her head, sits up straight, and begins to look around.*

Lying Left: *(To handbag)* What a lovely color! You look brand new. Is that so?

Opulence: No, not brand new. But I am used only on special occasions and manage to retain my poise and charm. Opulence, the handbag.

Lying Left: How lovely! Lying Left, the stocking.

Opulence: Pleased to meet you.

Lying Left: You must excuse me, but I cannot refrain from making a comment about your material texture. It is not often that I meet such well-done handbags. What a design! I can smell the leather from here. You must be over one hundred dollars.

Opulence: Three hundred fifty without taxes. You look quite exquisite as well, but to be honest, whenever I get to travel, I find myself surrounded by everything of a highest quality.

And therefore your appearance does not surprise me.

Lying Left: *(slightly offended and wishing to get back in a polite manner)* Forgive me for asking, but I always wondered if handbags got bored sitting around all day. I cannot imagine my life without constant motion.

Opulence: No, in fact I always wondered if socks and stockings get tired running around all day. I am lucky to have the privilege to always sit around or be carried around. You must be born into it.

Lying Left: I see. But isn't it hard to … well, meet others, if all you do is sit around?

Opulence: Why do I need the others? I am lucky to have been matched with Wealth, the leather wallet. I have had three partners before him, but they didn't have enough style. Wealth fits me perfectly, if you know what I mean.

Wealth: *(cheerfully)* She must mean I fit into her perfectly.

*Opulence is a little discomposed. Not sure how to react.*

Lying Left: *(quickly trying to continue the conversation)* You expect you both will live a long, happy life and get thrown out together?

Opulence: Oh, who thinks about that! I am so nice and expensive. I wouldn't be thrown out anytime soon.

Wise Right: *(addressing Wealth)* I am Wise Right. I notice you are quite potbellied. What kind of currency do you carry, if you do not mind me asking?

Wealth: Pleased to meet you. Wealth, the leather wallet. I carry about three hundred in dollars and euros, but mostly it's the credit cards. Such lovely, thin girls!

Wise Right: My judgment might deceive me, but you look unusually potbellied for a wallet.

Wealth: Oh, it must be the foreign coins. I give them all to my brother when I get back home. He holds a whole harem of coins from different parts of the world and periods of time.

Wise Right: You must know a great deal about coins.

Wealth: Yes, indeed I do.

Wise Right: That is very interesting. Do you also happen to know the current price of euros in dollars?

Wealth: That would not be a question for me. But if you please, I can call the Calculator to find out. He is always at my service. Such a diligent employee!

Opulence: I am getting sleepy. Wealth, honey, would anyone mind if I rest a little?

Wealth: Not at all, Opulence dear.

Lying Left: I am feeling a bit dozy as well.

Wise Right: No wonder. It's nighttime back home.

Lying Left: (*settling on the shoulder of Wise Right to sleep*)
Opulence is so lovely and stylish.

Wise Right: Wealth is quite interesting to talk to.

Lying Left: *(falling asleep)* Uh-huh

*Lights dim. All leave the stage carrying off the airplane setting.*

**END OF SCENE**

## SCENE 3

*Brightly lit empty stage. Five pairs stock-walk out on stage, four women (stockings) and six men (socks), each carrying a tall column. Columns are placed on the floor in a straight row. They represent chair legs and should be positioned appropriately. One pair of women is Wise Right and Lying Left. One woman from the other pair has holes in her dress. There is common chatter as everyone enters.*

Sock 1: Have you met Director Socks before?

Stocking 1: No, but I have heard so much about them.

Sock 2: They were with the company for over twenty years and are running pretty much everything.

Lying Left: I thought they were only the managers of ONE.

Stocking 2: No, Wasley was ONE manager, but ONE was split into four groups.

Sock 2: Director Socks might be managing only one group, but I know my managers don't do anything without Director Socks' approval.

*A pair of men, Director Socks, stock-walk onto the stage, each carrying a column. Everyone stops chatting and takes their places in-between the columns they brought in, where the feet of sitting people would be. Director Socks place the columns on the side of the stage, at a right angle to the row of columns, as if forming two sides of the table with Director Socks at the head.*

*Lying Left, being next to the other pair of stockings, suddenly falls to her knees. All turn to her and notice the holes on Stocking 2, nodding disapproval. Lying Left now gets up, nice and straight, while embarrassed Stocking 2 tries to hide behind her pair-mate.*

Wise Right: *(aside to Lying Left)* That was quite unmerciful.

Lying Left: *(aside to Wise Right)* Uh, if it wasn't for me, you would never get anywhere. She was struck by the arrow of holes, and she wouldn't last long anyway. In one move, I made sure everyone noticed how good I am and put that pair out of the game.

Wise Right: *(aside to Lying Left)* But they'll be thrown out soon. No one stays after they get struck by the arrow. You had to make it worse. Everyone sees your cruelty. It is unwise to earn such a reputation. It will backfire in the end.

Lying Left: *(aside to Wise Right)* So far it has worked just fine.

*As the speech begins, all socks and stockings are silent and motionless.*

Voice: (*male, serious, well-paced, loud and clear but monotonous*) Thank you all for coming. I am very happy to take advantage of this opportunity to inform you of our ongoing BVMUR project that was originally started by the ONE group under

Wasley. Those developers have done a great job of building the base for this effort by creating initial guidelines.

*All but Director Socks and Wise Right can begin to shift from side to side, as they would move with the feet during a long and boring speech. Director Socks and Wise Right remain serious and still.*

Voice: Today's meeting is the first of the series planned by higher management for the purpose of informing other departments of the ongoing work that has been done to improve our environment. We are making every possible effort to prepare you all for the upcoming changes that will take effect after the roll-out date that has been scheduled for August 2007, three years from now. I am pleased to see all of you taking time to participate. Your presence shows your initiative and your interest in the future that is essential for success.

*As the Voice proceeds with the speech, a man dressed in brown runs out on stage with the words—Falling, falling, falling. He falls next to one of the socks or stockings, assuming a twisted position to represent an accidentally dropped Pretzel. The stockings light up with evil smiles and short, evil laughs, except for the Wise Right and Director Socks. During the rest of the speech, socks and stockings try to step on the Pretzel as he awkwardly moves away from one offender just to end up in the area within reach of the other. He might make offended, helpless sounds and look miserable as he tries to escape.*

Voice: To give you a brief history of the BVMUR project—as I already mentioned, it originated with ONE group in an effort to deal with the N&B problem that arose due to the clash of TYI and HJO, both of which are essential to keep the EQSY running. You will recall that ONE group was split right after the rollout of EQSY into four groups: LDL, RDL, LWL, and RWR to support TYI and HJO. Four months later it was decided to combine RDL with RWL into one group: RDW, which I am a manager of. BVMUR was given to us three months ago.

Consolidating nodes and migrating decommissioned attribute repository in our best efforts preferred by management. It is an iterative process, as we move from stage one to stage five, stages two and four being our break-points when we put our new rules into effect and see them live in the production environment before continuing with the developmental process. We leverage their expertise in the area of aggregate consolidation to combine nodes in iterative process production rollout, stages three and five being intermediate. New resources allocated, client satisfaction, taking out best efforts, management support, hard work of our team members.

We will save four million after three years after stage two goes to production. In one year, after stage two goes to production, we project to complete implementation of stage three. In two years, after stage two goes live, we will have stage four ready for rollout. At this time, we will have developed appropriate metrics to measure the quality of BVMUR performance, and we will also have collected sufficient data describing performance of stage two that will now enter the maintenance phase as stages three and four enter production phase. It follows that in three years we will have stages one and two in corrective development, three and four in production and stage five in initial development. To summarize, we will save ten million just in five years from today. We will need resources provided by other departments, and this is where you guys come in. After completion of stage one, we will produce the roadmap that the rest of our efforts will follow, and we will make our best efforts to keep you informed of our further development and any modifications to the original plan that you received as you came in.

*Several men and women dressed in white to represent accidentally dropped plan pages run out chanting their page numbers—two, seventy, fifty-nine, twenty-five, one hundred sixteen, etc. They fall down all over. One of the socks or stockings, with a satisfied, evil smile, finally steps on the Pretzel and a piece of his costume falls off. In the confusion of all the pages, he is able to escape.*

Voice: Once again, I thank you all for coming. Spread the word to your colleagues. The next BVMUR information session will be held on Monday of next week.

*Socks and stockings can begin to move around, pushing the chanting pages aside. Director Socks approach Lying Left and Wise Right.*

Director Sock 1: *(clearly addressing Lying Left)* I heard your presentation last week at the BNS meeting.

Director Sock 2: *(clearly addressing Lying Left)* I remember you addressed some interesting points.

Director Sock 1: Say we have dinner together. Are you free tonight?

Wise Right: *(aside to Lying Left)* Don't do this, you will regret it later.

Lying Left: *(aside to Wise Right)* We are doing it, and there is nothing you can do about it. We've made an agreement to alternate demands. Last Friday we stayed at work until 10:00 p.m. on your demand. Now it is my turn to demand, and you know you cannot refuse.

*(To Director Socks)* Yes, actually, we are free tonight and will gladly accept your invitation.

*Lights begin dimming to ruby twilight and classically romantic French melody begins to play, first softly then louder, as all but Director Socks, Wise Right, and Lying Left leave the stage carrying off the columns.*

**END OF SCENE**

## SCENE 4

*Director Socks dance with Wise Right and Lying Left. Lying Left dances passionately and beautifully with both socks while Wise Right uncomfortably shifts from side to side, being unwanted but unable to leave. The dance movements should not violate the fact that socks and stockings are moving with the feet. At the end of the dance, Director Socks, Wise Right, and Lying Left fall onto the stage, one by one, as if being taken off and thrown on the floor.*

*Ruby light darkens; music continues playing, slowly changing into alarming sounds of danger mixed with loud vacuum cleaner noise. A man dressed in an enormous dark cloak, the vacuum cleaner, enters. He chases after socks and stockings, has a violent struggle with one of the Director Socks, hurts Wise Right, hides Lying Left under his cloak, and leaves the stage with her.*

*Lights dim to black.*

**END OF SCENE**

**SCENE 5**

*Bars are constructed on the stage, as in scene one. Lighting is dim, amber, mysterious. Dreamy Right and Wise Right are "hanging" on the bars.*

Dreamy Right: *(horrified)* The vacuum cleaner?

Wise Right: Yes, in the morning, the vacuum cleaner came in and … Lying Left was gone within seconds. He tried to get one of the Director Socks as well, but socks are tougher than us and cannot be swallowed so easily. That's where I got my scar.

*(Pause)*

Then I was brought home, washed, stitched, and put away in the drawer. For so long! So long! I know it is not my fault. There was nothing I could have done, but all the same, I feel so much pain. The hurt. The constant, aching hurt.

Dreamy Right: The continuous, aching hurt.

Wise Right: What would you know about it?

Dreamy Right: You are not being fair. I lost my Lovely Left too.

Wise Right: I lost everything. No more late evenings at work. No more interesting encounters. No stimulating discussions. No … Lying Left. She might have been cruel to others sometimes, but we understood each other. And … always loved each other.

*(Pause)*

Now I have to be here, with you. Always listening about your emotions, fantasies, impressions, associations, abstractions. Why should you be unhappy? Every Friday we get to go to that dull bar, listen to that awful, noisy music, and come home smelling of beer and cigarettes. One day that ash will burn one of us. That is your life. That is what you've always been doing. Yes, you lost your pair-mate, but you still have your life. I have nothing. There is nothing for me to talk about with the socks that hang around that place. I am sorry I was ever taken out of the drawer. At least it was clean there.

<u>Dreamy Right</u>: *(quietly, talking with difficulty)* These evenings that we have now are not at all like the evenings that were then, before Lovely Left was gone. They were full of laughter and dancing. We hardly dance anymore. Yesterday, we were invited only once, and those socks looked so bored with us.

<u>Wise Right</u>: Of course they were bored. They like to be entertained. I, of course, wouldn't even think of laughing at any of those disgusting, dirty jokes that go around in that place, forget about repeating them. And you were simply lost in the music, in the memories, or whatever else you get lost in.

<u>Dreamy Right</u>: Oh, I miss my Lovely Left so much. It feels like all the merriment, the spirit of celebration went with her. I can tell you about those days, but I am sure you won't

understand. You are too … wise for it.

*(Pause)*

So listen.

*Lights dim to black. Bars are carried off the stage.*

**END OF SCENE**

## SCENE 6

*Bright light. Dreamy Right and Lovely Left lie on the floor center stage.*

Lovely Left: It should be about time. My Dreamy Right, we are going out tonight!

Dreamy Right: You are always right about these things. How do you do it, my Lovely Left?

*Lovely Left starts to get up—gracefully, sexy. Dreamy Right looks at her with fascination.*

Lovely Left: What did I tell you? We are going out tonight!

Dreamy Right: What did I tell you? You are always right!

*Dreamy Right gets up awkwardly. Now both stand side-by-side. Movements of Lovely Left are graceful, enthusiastic, full of energy. Dreamy Right moves and gestures exaggeratedly slow, dreamily.*

Lovely Left: *(loudly)* It's party time!

Dreamy Right: *(like an echo)* Party time!

*They stock-walk off stage. As soon as they exit, lights dim and the stage is filled with heavy smoke. A loud shutting-the-door sound is heard. Dreamy Right and*

*Lovely Left reenter. They stock-walk toward the stage exit on the opposite side. The pace should be slow enough to complete the conversation before reaching the exit.*

Lovely Left: *(irritably)* What a weather today. Warm and clear summer evenings were so good. And it will get worse from here—first it's chilly autumn, then it's freezy winter.

Dreamy Right: *(getting more and more animated as she speaks)* It's the fog! Can't you feel how much more interesting it is to walk in the fog? You are always thinking only of the party. Don't worry—we'll get there. These are probably the most fascinating moments of the evening—the way to the party. Notice how different the familiar road looks. In this fog, we are in the magic kingdom—the world where anything is possible. We are hidden from reality by this dark, watery shawl.

*(Perhaps makes a movement of wrapping herself in the fog)*

It's all around us, it hides us, it touches us, it fills us.

*(takes a deep breath)*

We are walking within the amazing; we are the ghosts wandering through the meaning of life. At moments like these, I feel like I am touching the purpose of life. I don't grasp it. I don't understand it. I touch it. Or rather it touches me, like this fog. It's all around, it's watery and it's light, and I can feel its tiny drops. And I can breathe it. But I cannot take it. I cannot keep it. I can only feel it. And this is sensational. This is worth everything in life. This is life itself!

Lovely Left: Uh-huh. I hope we'll see Grey Stripes tonight.

*Both stockings exit.*

**END OF SCENE**

## SCENE 7

*Light is dim but brighter than before. Fog slowly settles down. Dance music is playing—low enough not to be a distraction, but loud enough for all to speak in raised voices. One side of the stage is a dance floor. Jazz Socks are dancing with a pair of stockings, not violating the restricted set of moves possible to them, since they are moving with the feet.*

*Something to lean against is constructed on the other side of the stage—the base of the bar counter. Two stockings (women)—Best Friend One and Best Friend Two, an Umbrella (a man), a Rain Coat (a woman), a Crazy Ring (a woman) are standing next to or leaning against the base of the bar counter.*

*Dreamy Right and Lovely Left enter.*

Dreamy Right: So crowded. Where will we sit? What do we do?

Lovely Left: I really don't understand you. We've been to this place so many times, and every time you become nervous when we come in. Who cares where we sit? We can sit anywhere! Besides, I see Best Friends over there by the counter. Let's go say hi.

Dreamy Right: *(relieved)* Right, of course. Let's go.

Best Friend One: Lovely Left! Come on up here!

Best Friend Two: What's happening? Haven't seen you in a week.

You look lovely!

*All four hug. Umbrella and Rain Coat are whispering and tenderly hugging each other.*

Best Friend One: *(motioning to Umbrella and Rain Coat)* These are Umbrella and Rain Coat, they came in with those stockings on the dance floor.

Lovely Left: Hi, I'm Lovely Left.

Dreamy Right: Dreamy Right.

*The sound of chin-chinked glasses is heard and something resembling spilled liquid falls down. Lovely Left glides her finger across the floor and tastes it.*

Lovely Left: Beer.

*Dreamy Right and Best Friends follow her motions.*

Best Friend One: Not Bad.

Best Friend Two: Not bad at all.

Lovely Left: Such a weather today. I am happy you made it here. Have you seen Grey Stripes? Oh, I so hope they'll come by.

Umbrella: Weather? The weather is great! If it wasn't for such weather, me and my sweet Rain Coat would never meet.

Best Friend One: They were just about to tell us how they met for the first time. Start from the beginning.

Umbrella: How about Rain Coat tells her version of our first date.

Rain Coat: No, you tell it better. I want to listen.

Umbrella: All right. It was an exceptional day. Exceptional because I was taken off the top shelf where I usually reside for weeks. What a great rain poured down that day! Not the small, drizzly one, but a great, grand rain! And a mighty wind too. I spread out my wings and looked up at the sky, facing the oceans of water coming down on me. Zigzags of lightning blinded the black sky, one after the other. And did I squint once? No. I've done my squinting in the days long past. I could now openly, fearlessly enjoy the full force of the raging nature. I felt every drop as it hit my wings, and I wished it was even stronger. I wanted more! It was a rough rain, but it made me hunger for more. Suddenly, I became aware of the noise hardly audible in the groans of thunder. It was the Rain Coat, my dear Rainy, and she was crying. She was new and worn for the first time. Of course, she was afraid. Especially of a rain like that. And I must confess of being careless. I was completely engulfed in my own triumphant flight through the storm. I let the wind wave me from side to side, leaving her unprotected from the mighty, wet blows. I lowered my eyes. Looked at her. I talked to her. I told her not to be scared. I told her the rain was to be enjoyed, not feared. I steadied myself and shielded her from the storm.

*Glasses chin-chink again and something resembling liquid pours down. All taste it as Umbrella continues.*

Umbrella: Then we spent two hours in the darkness of the theater. She calmed down. Even smiled. What a beautiful smile you have, Rainy. Looking at that smile, I knew that I could never enjoy a single rain without you. I thought I knew all the possible pleasures the rain could offer, but I was wrong. I want to protect you with my wings from all the storms that might frighten you. I want to see you smile and play in the drizzly weather. Without you, any weather is sunshine and I am useless. I love you, my Rain Coat.

Rain Coat: I love you. I love you. Ever since we met in that storm for the first time, I could not stop thinking of you. Such a long time passed until we met again. I … I thought that you forgot all about me. I was afraid that we would never meet again. I tried to forget all about it, but I just couldn't. I waited. Every day I hoped for rain.

Umbrella: Yes, we don't get to see each other too often. But when we do, these days are true gifts of life. Like today. Today is amazing. Today is exceptional.

*Glasses chin-chink, liquid pours down.*

Crazy Ring: *(suddenly and loudly)* Let's imagine, one day you actually decided to do it. Of course, you wouldn't, but imagine you did. And why wouldn't you? Everyone's life should have some exceptional incidents. If one's life consists of many exceptions, it's an exceptional life, but the ordinary ones shouldn't get too jealous. After all, too many exceptions can become accepted as natural and that would lessen the intensity of excitement experienced at its peak when a truly ordinary someone decides to take a truly exceptional course of action during a period of his truly ordinary life. I think it's best if I preserve your anonymity by calling you Exception. So listen up, you are about to learn about your own exceptional experience.

It all started in the morning, at 5:00 a.m. to be exact—I know how you like to be exact, and since I am trying to please you I will also be exact. The alarm clock larmed loudly—AM-AM-AM-AM-AM-AM—and you found yourself standing in the middle of the room, half naked, cold, and hardly awake, in other words quite miserable, which is normal. It was Wednesday, which is normal too. But you weren't in your room, and it wasn't your alarm clock, although it had a similar larm. But wait, something is wrong. If you are already in my room, that means the exceptional experience has already happened. Where did I get off track? Aha! I was telling you about the morning. I should have started with the morning on Tuesday when you decided not to buy a newspaper because … Wait a second. Did I already say it was my room? Uh, yes I did. Well, don't get any wrong ideas. It's not about that, and it's not like that. As I said, this is an exceptional story, so don't think along the ordinary lines of he plus she in her room. This is more about the alarm clock than about he or she. Did I say it was about the alarm clock? Oy—I am giving away all the secrets. I guess I won't be able to intrigue you. Actually, now that I ruined the story, I no longer feel like telling it. So get dressed and leave like all of them—exceptional minds with most ordinary needs. Who spends the night with her bringing his own alarm clock so he can be at work on time the next day? What? Oh, right. This is your room. So I got a little carried away. Don't worry. I am leaving. And turn that alarm off! What? It's five thirty already? How did I manage to fall asleep while standing in the middle of the room, cold and miserable? Oh, I am not standing. I am still in bed. My alarm is still larming? Have to turn it off. Where are you? Oh, I am all alone, I forgot. It's Five oh five. Good. I thought I was late.

*All stare in confusion.*

Rain Coat: Don't mind her. She's a Crazy Ring. She always tells these tales that go round and round in circles but always revolve around the alarm clock. Poor thing. Whether home or elsewhere, she always gets to sleep next to the alarm clock. What an unhealthy relationship. Apparently, daily early wake-up rings drove the Ring crazy.

*Glasses chin-chink, liquid pours down.*

Lovely Left: Have you noticed that as the night progresses, more and more is getting spilled?

*(after trying the liquid)*

Guys, this is no beer. This is vodka!

Best Friend One: All right!

Best Friend Two: Let's try it!

Lovely Left: What type of socks you like best?

Best Friend One: Oh, I like my socks to be light with colorful ornaments. I hate plain, pale socks. Nothing to look at. What about you?

Lovely Left: I like my socks to have stripes. Never the circles. Circles suck.

Best Friend Two: You know, last week … Aw, that was so cool! It was very cold in the evening …

Best Friend One: It was cold and we got socks put on over us.

Best Friend Two: That was so awesome!

Best Friend One: It was so weird! To walk around with socks on top of us.

Lovely Left: Were they the ones with green triangles?

Best Friend One: No, you don't know them. They had penguins on them. They are house socks, very thick and warm.

Dreamy Right: *(suddenly and awkwardly breaking her silence)* And I had lunch with Wild Wool Socks. You know, wool socks, the ones with messy, loose loops and strands sticking out in all directions.

Best Friend Two: The Wild Wool?

Dreamy Right: Yes.

Best Friend One: Wow! You rock! Tell us what happened?

*Dreamy Right is embarrassed and lost. Lovely Left gives her angry looks.*

Best Friend Two: Are you meeting again? When?

Dreamy Right: Ummmm … maybe.

Best Friend One: Come on, tell us all!

*Jazz Socks stock-walk from the dance area and pass by Lovely Left. She lightly pushes one of them.*

Jazz Sock One: Hey, did you poke my heel?

Lovely Left: That's the worst pick-up line ever.

Jazz Sock Two: If it's the pick-up line, then it's yours. I saw you poke him.

Lovely Left: Fine, I'm not going to dance with you.

Jazz Sock Two: Then let's go dancing, beautiful!

*Lovely Left, Dreamy Right, and Jazz Socks stock-walk to the dance floor. Music is played louder. They dance. Then the music volume is turned down and they stock-walk back to the bar counter.*

Jazz Sock One: You are lovely.

Lovely Left: *(playfully)* You want to know a secret? You do? You do? You really do? Naturally I am blond, but I was dyed beige to look more sophisticated. When I was blond, whenever I came out of the house, all the socks would run after me. That became so annoying.

Jazz Sock Two: You are incredible. I am giving a jazz concert tomorrow night. Come down. We'll chat.

Lovely Left: I'll think about it, Jazzy. But I must split for the night. Later. *(To Best Friends)* I'll see you guys next week, as usual. *(To Umbrella and Rain Coat, who are still hugging and whispering to each other)* I hope I'll see you here, on rainy nights. *(To all)* Take care, good night.

*Lights are dimmed. Music stops. Bar settings are carried off stage.*

**END OF SCENE**

## SCENE 8

*Dim lights. Fog fills the stage. Lovely Left and Dreamy Right enter. Their stock-walking should clearly demonstrate the effects of drinking. Perhaps one or both should fall.*

Lovely Left: Why did you have to bring up Wild Wool?

Dreamy Right: Oh, I don't know. I felt so stupid being silent the whole time while everyone chatted about their experiences. This was the only one thing I could have said and so I said it. Let's not talk about it.

Lovely Left: You shouldn't have said it. There are socks that you chat about in the bar and there are socks that you never talk about. To anyone. Ever. You keep it to yourself.

Dreamy Right: You are right. I will never, never talk about that which must stay in the privacy of dreams. I felt awful the moment I said it. And all of them with their questions I didn't want to answer. I was totally lost.

Lovely Left: Thank me for rescuing you out of it.

Dreamy Right: How do you always know the correct, the conventionally, the socially accepted way of behaving? You know where to sit, what to do, what to say. You are always right. I never know what to say and when.

Lovely Left: That's why you leave that part to me.

Dreamy Right: *(in a sudden, absolute desperation)* But what should I do now? I feel awful. Just awful. I can't go on like this. Do something! Anything!

Lovely Left: What you do is promise yourself to never do it again.

*Lovely Left patronizingly offers her arms for a hug. They hug.*

Dreamy Right: I can't believe I've talked about him.

*(Pause)*

Do you think I should tell him?

Lovely Left: You want to talk to him about your talking about him? Haven't you done enough of unnecessary talking already?

Dreamy Right: No, I mean tell him I like him … very much?

Lovely Left: Oh. You do know that you are no match for him?

Dreamy Right: I am not trying to be a match for him. It's just that there are not a lot of socks that I'd have a crush on and I want him to know that he is amazing. I am not thinking of a possibility of a relationship. That is impossible.

*(Pause)*

Wild Wool is not like any other sock I've ever met. The Left

Wild Wool … He is of such unique quality. So warm and strong are his threads. And all those loose loops and strands sticking out in messy confusion! He is no standard mass-manufactured sock. He is amazing! I must find a creative way of letting him know.

Lovely Left: You are getting out of the conventional realm. I can be of no help to you there. Prepare to be embarrassed and miserable.

Dreamy Right: I've already had a lot of practice in both.

Lovely Left: Too bad Grey Stripes didn't come out tonight. I was hoping.

Dreamy Right: We'll be washed tomorrow.

Lovely Left: And worn again next Saturday.

*A pair of socks, Grey Stripes, enters and stock-runs to catch up with Dreamy Right and Lovely Left as the stockings are about to exit the stage.*

Grey Stripe One: *(panting after running)* Hey, I am sorry we couldn't come out earlier.

Grey Stripe Two: We came by the bar and they told us you just left.

Grey Stripe One: Listen, I wanted to tell you for a while now, but couldn't. I … We've known each other for quite some time now. And … Well, I keep thinking of you. And I think that you think about me as well. I can spend another night watching TV and thinking of you. And you will be all alone too. So how about we just go watch TV together.

Dreamy Right: *(aside to Lovely Left)* Oh, no. No! Please no!

Lovely Left: *(aside to Dreamy Right)* Did you hear the story of Umbrella and Rain Coat? I want to be loved too. This is real. Grey Stripes are here and now and possible. I cannot live in the dream world like you, however beautiful it is. Dreams and life are different.

Dreamy Right: *(aside to Lovely Left)* I want to live a dream.

Lovely Left: *(aside to Dreamy Right)* You want to live in a dream and I want to live in life. *(to Grey Stripes)* I … I have been thinking of you too.

*Lovely Left leans toward Grey Stripe One for a kiss. Dreamy Right struggles with Grey Stripe Two but is also kissed.*

Grey Stripe One: My house is only two blocks down.

Lovely Left: Lead the way.

*All exit. Lights dim to black.*

**END OF SCENE**

## SCENE 9

*Bars on stage, as in scenes one and five. Lighting is dim, amber, mysterious. Dreamy Right and Wise Right are "hanging" on the bars.*

Wise Right: What happened next?

Dreamy Right: I don't want to talk about it. I don't want to think about it. I don't. I don't. I just don't.

Wise Right: What happened next?

Dreamy Right: What do you care? Leave me alone. I hate you.

Wise Right: What happened next?

Dreamy Right: Stop asking me. I am not talking about it.

*(Pause)*

They kept my Lovely Left. I was brought home alone. I … I didn't, I couldn't even believe it. All the time I thought that I would turn around and there she would be, next to me. But there was no one next to me. I was washed, placed in the drawer next to you. The strangest thing was that I could not even dream anymore. I used to lose myself in my fantasies for hours. But in the drawer, having all the time in the world, I could imagine nothing. All was emptiness and pain. You never talked to me, though. Not until we were taken out and worn together.

Wise Right: I was preoccupied with my own grief. Besides, I never heard you crying.

Dreamy Right: Crying? I never cry. Maybe it would be easier if I could.

Wise Right: I could never cry either. No matter what.

Dreamy Right: The hurt. The constant, aching hurt.

Wise Right: The continuous, aching hurt.

Dreamy Right: And this place that we visit every Friday. I do not know anybody there. I don't know why we keep going there. To sit all by ourselves. For hours. Just sit and wait. For what?

Wise Right: Yes, our former pair-mates knew how to live. All we can do is think and dream.

Dreamy Right: Lying and Lovely left. What do we do now?

Wise Right: I will think. You will dream.

Dreamy Right: And we can tell stories. Wise Right! How about we tell our stories? Tell them to anyone we meet who is willing to listen.

Wise Right: Hmm. That sounds interesting.

Dreamy Right: In our stories, can we distort the facts or add imaginary ones? Can we talk of what we fear or desire the most as of true facts we lived through?

Wise Right: I don't see why not.

Dreamy Right: Then we'll make our story different every time! We'll gather a big crowd around us next Friday. And all the Fridays to come!

Wise Right: Wait, wait, don't get too excited beforehand.

Dreamy Right: I love you, Wise Right. I know I said I hate you many times, but I didn't really mean it. Well, maybe I meant it when I said it, but I don't mean it in general. You let me fly and fall, but you keep me from burning either on the sun or in the earth's core.

Wise Right: I love you, Dreamy Right. I scold you often, but I'd never wish you to change. Stay as you are with all your dreams free of logic and wisdom. Stay this way, and bear with my comments that might, at times, be useful.

*Wise Right patronizingly offers her arms for a hug. Dreamy Right readily accepts.*

Wise Right: Now let's work on our first story.

Dreamy Right: And make humans our main characters.

**END OF SCENE**

**CURTAIN**

MICHAEL CHEVAL 2007

# *Takeoff*

There she stood, her eyes behind the glasses. A soft figure he'd like to press against with a "mmmm, mmmy darling" into her ear. Her shoulder-long, incredibly blond, naturally or not he could not tell, hair added an erotic radiance to her young, intelligent face. How old was she? End of high school? Beginning of college? She must be in the fascinating period of adult conscience fresh with adolescent wonder. A nightmare for young professors. She must be a good student. He wanted her to be. A brilliant straight-A girl with an intricate web of relationships in her private life. She'd take flawless notes in her history class while writing a dirty letter to her boyfriend, who sits one row behind. She'd turn around, pretending to check something in his textbook, and slip the letter onto his desk. As he reads it, she will raise her hand to describe the powerful forces of nature that scattered the Spanish Armada in 1588. And into her speech she will incorporate some of the words she used in her letter, pronouncing them in commonplace calm so that no one suspects the double meaning they have for the boyfriend. The powerful forces of nature will cause the boy to experience his own storm, and when the bell rings, he is embarrassed to get up as he watches the blond teaser leave the room, not giving him so much as a glance.

The St. Petersburg-Paris plane was three hours delayed. Not only did it cause present inconvenience, but also promised even bigger troubles of being late for the Paris-New York connection. Everything in the airport seemed unpleasant, even threatening. Everything besides the blond girl's soft curves. The dull, brown seats, the multitude of faces, each repulsive in its own way—some sharply annoyed, some brick-wall bored, some distorted by disturbed sleep, some still wet with goodbye tears. Everything was marked with suppressed fear of the flight itself, of the dangers ahead. But the girl, she knows better than to be bored or scared. She is smart enough not to worry about things she cannot control. She is too preoccupied with her own sexuality to be bored. The way she playfully runs her long fingers through her hair. She knows that he is secretly watching her. She knows that half of the waiting passengers are secretly watching her.

From the corner of his eye, he observed an elderly man, probably a grandfather, approaching the girl, dimming her glowing appeal with a shadow of disappointment. She was accompanied. It would prevent him from starting even the most innocent conversation. Still, the girl was attractive. Why didn't she wear a skirt? Why did she hide herself behind that business-casual suit outfit? That blond teaser!

The girl's serious composure broke into animated lines when the cell phone sounded from the depths of her small handbag. After digging it out with her kissable fingers, she put the phone to her delicate ear. A smile of recognition. She did not say very much, only listened with occasional ahas. Aha! It must be one of her boyfriends. He must be caressing her ear with the words of wild, erotic fantasies while she is caught in a situation where being next to her grandfather she cannot answer, only listen. Sure she could get up and walk to the far end of the airport, but she liked being placed in this position; she was experimenting with the thrill of it, tasting the extent of presented limitation.

Maybe, in a way, it was really he who was calling her, in his mind, through the means of the boyfriend. "Hi, darling. My dear, sexy, blond teaser. You are in the airport now?"

"Aha," she said.

"Mmmm, pretend I am next to you. Would you like me to be next to you?"

"Aha," she repeated.

"Imagine you are sitting on my lap, honey. I blow on your hair and I kiss your neck. I am holding you, pressing you to me. You take my hand and guide it under your blouse. You are not wearing a bra, you naughty you!" The girl crossed her legs in response. "I want every lovely part of you; I caress every sexy curve; I kiss every cavity. I want you to touch yourself, for me, pretend that it's me." The girl squeezed her legs, slightly, barely noticeable. "That's right, my blond teaser, my dear sex goddess." He would have liked it so much to take her glasses off and look within, to dishevel her suit open and touch inside.

Just as he was about to move into areas more private, the girl hung up the phone and placed it back in her handbag. There was still an hour-long wait ahead. He got up and headed to the airport café for some wine.

* * *

Alexandra walked ahead of her grandfather into the plane and took a seat next to the window. Her back straight and tense, she stared at the blue material of the seat in front, focusing on the vibrations of the airplane, preparing to be terrified. She had been through too many flights to keep an accurate account of, but every time it was the same. It was more than the fear of accidents, though this fear took up a large portion of Alexandra's airplane terror pie chart. She was overly sensitive to the lifts and falls through the air during the first few minutes of takeoff. Overcome by uncontrollable fright, she grabbed and squeezed anything within reach. Her parents and grandparents always abandoned her in these seizures of panic, considering them silly, and keeping their hands away. The rest of the flight was spent in the anxious anticipation to get through it. Even the intervals of heavy turbulence were not as bad as the takeoff.

"I told you not to buy that book. Now, what if we have to spend days waiting for another plane to take us from Paris to home? You never think ahead. I always tell you, you must think ahead to avoid getting into these situations," said Alexandra's grandfather in Russian. She ignored the comment and he continued, "It was probably more expensive in the airport than if you had bought it in a regular bookstore when we got home. You must learn to curb your wants and think about the needs at present."

"My need at present is to survive the takeoff," Alexandra answered.

"Stop this foolishness; you are not a baby anymore. Look around you. The airplane is full of people. Everyone behaves normally. Look at that man; he is sitting and reading. Not only did you waste money, you did not even open your book."

Alexandra's eyes followed in the direction of the middle row of triple seats her grandfather pointed to. There sat a man, about the age of forty, reading the exact same book she had bought.

Head pressed hard into the back of her seat, eyes locked on the whiteness of the page framed in the corner by the man's hand, Alexandra suffered the takeoff. Up-up-up-up-up—her hands grabbed the little blue pillow, muscles tensed, fingers locked. Down-down-down-down-down—just when she could not take one more down, the plane stabilized, giving her a few moments of relief before the next series of lifts and falls. During one of such relieves, Alexandra became aware, for the first time, of the reading man's raspberry-colored shirt, his big shoulders, his broad chest. The hand supporting his book seemed strong and manly and capable. Capable of what? Of caressing her face, of running tenderly through her hair, of reassuring her, of making her unafraid. By the time the "Fasten Your Seatbelt" sign was off, Alexandra's imagination placed her beside the man. She was tightly cuddled against him, her face buried in his shoulder, his hand embracing her, his soothing words telling her not to be scared.

Alexandra reached for her book. The man was many pages ahead of her.

* * *

About two hours later, on her way back from the restroom, Alexandra made a decision in a snap of a second. It was the right moment. Whenever she was not entangled in the sticky web of awkward shyness that sometimes descended upon her, Alexandra could be very direct. She stopped by the reading man's seat and looked over his shoulder at the book.

"So what happens on the two-forty-forth page?" she heard herself address him in English. The man looked up immediately, as though he couldn't wait to be interrupted by the girl's voice. "I am reading the same book. Up to one-eighteenth," she added when their eyes met.

The man spent a few leisurely seconds regarding Alexandra's form. "How are you liking it?" he finally answered.

"I? I like it, but I. I originally thought it would be more serious," said Alexandra, realizing that she was not prepared to discuss the book.

"More serious? How so? This is one of the most serious books I've ever read," challenged the man.

"Well, it's about World War II. I'd expect it to have more; I mean, all the characters walk around hating their circumstances, telling dirty jokes, disclosing stories about their girlfriends, cursing continuously, instead of being proud to fight for their country," Alexandra finally squeezed out of herself.

The man was only half interested in her answers. What most captivated him was the curious accent. The original model he created of her in his mind had perfect diction, but the true sound made her even more interesting. Her speech added an exotic twist to her erotic radiance. "But would you be interested in reading the book if it did not have all those titillating details?" he continued.

Alexandra did not know what the word titillating meant, and her cheeks began to burn. She felt as if she was under attack with questions for bullets. "I don't know. I guess not. But I mean. None of them ever even mention the cause, the main purpose of their fighting, the big picture," she answered, feeling ashamed for the quivering in her voice.

"Ah, so you consider the reasons for the war presented by government to be bigger than the lives and thoughts of individuals fighting the war?" continued the man in his calm, interested fashion.

"But what about patriotism?" Alexandra felt on the verge of something, she did not know what.

"Patriotism? That's nothing. That's stupidity," said the man.

Alexandra did not know what to say next and hurried to excuse herself with, "I guess I should get back to the book. I've read so little of it that I don't have the right to discuss it."

"All right, then. It was a pleasure talking to you." The man extended his hand for a handshake. Feeling his gentle squeeze, Alexandra became aware of her pounding heart.

The man returned to his book. Alexandra waited for her grandfather to get up and let her through to her seat. She was finally safe, shielded from strange questions. How could he say patriotism is stupidity?

As a child, Alexandra watched many Russian WWII movies, where young men were proud to defend their country, their loved ones back home. During the hours of rest, they wrote beautiful letters to their girlfriends and mothers. And when the young men died with proud songs on their lips, their friends were filled with noble sadness, not haunted at night with violent images of horror and disgust. There was no cursing, no hating, no confusion, degradation, or dirt. One scenario stood out especially clear and tragic in Alexandra's memory. A young man and a woman, both soldiers, fell in love during the course of the war. The circumstances led them apart, and the next time they met, they stood on the opposite sides of the minefield. But only the young man knew about the mines. With all his might, he yelled, trying to stop his lady soldier. But the noise of an airplane, passing overhead, drowned his words. The young lady soldier, drunk with happiness, thought he was calling her to him, and she ran, she ran, and blew up a few meters away from a kiss.

Alexandra did not want to read anymore. Neither did she want to talk to the reading man. It was far better to look at him and to think of him. She settled to sleep with the blue blanket comfortably tucked around her body. She and the reading man just barely escaped the enemy. Her shoulder was lightly wounded and he took care of her. They were safe in a tent. Just the two of them. Alexandra fell into the tender sweetness of sleep.

* * *

As they approached Paris, the atmosphere throughout the

airplane became loaded with concerns about missing the connecting flight to New York. Some passengers expressed hopes that due to the delay of their flight, the other plane would wait for them. Others smiled sarcastically at such naiveté. After a successful landing, the majority hurried to get out even faster than usual. Alexandra resisted her grandfather's attempts to rush her. She wanted to celebrate the landing by savoring the temporary relief. As she released her tension into an especially sweet sigh, stretching her hands up above her head, her eyes met the eyes of the reading man. He smiled and nodded goodbye before turning away to walk down the aisle. The immediate urge to catch up sharply transformed Alexandra's relaxed disposition. Soon her grandfather and she stood in a large airport hall looking at the administrator's desk surrounded by irritated clamor. The New York plane had taken off on schedule, two hours earlier.

The grandfather, who barely spoke English even though he had lived in New York for as long as Alexandra, was pushing her into the mass of people to find out what they must do next. Alexandra took small steps through the crowd, realizing that she would never push her way to the administrator. A large, portly man stood right near the desk, yelling curses in Russian and English, connecting them in a surprisingly skillful fashion. A woman next to him, possibly his wife, loudly explained that they were late to a wedding. Others, concerned with their own problems, agitatedly narrated their stories to whoever stood next to them. A short man with swollen, ruddy eyelids wondered where his baggage was. A middle-aged woman with an oversized yellow rose on an otherwise ordinary hat threatened with a lawsuit. Others begged the administrator to step into their shoes and be a human being enough to understand their unique circumstances. There was also an elderly lady breathing heavily as the younger woman, apparently her daughter, waved a magazine in front of her face to give her more air. Alexandra searched for the man in the raspberry shirt, but he was nowhere in sight.

Despite her grandfather's urgings, Alexandra never got to talk to the administrator, but in about forty minutes, the situation was resolved. An additional plane would be provided the next day in the afternoon. Alexandra looked at the round clock on the wall. It was almost eight in the evening. Everyone had to spend the night at the airport.

* * *

Slowly, the passengers settled into shiny, metallic seats. They were uncomfortable, but at least there was enough space for everybody. Alexandra's grandfather took out his worn-out learn-English kit, and she had nothing else to do but take off exploring the airport.

There were stores and restaurants, everything glittering. Wishing to escape from the busy crowd, Alexandra descended the flight of stairs, and then walked up a different one. She followed the wide, empty hallway until it ended in a passage into another narrower hallway. Was she allowed to go there? There weren't any guards around to stop her. Alexandra walked on, discovering a tiny waiting room much smaller than the one occupied by the passengers of her flight. The seats here were soft with brown leather and had high backs to lean on. There were only two men and a woman sitting far apart from each other. One of the men was wearing a raspberry shirt and looked straight at Alexandra in an engaging manner she had to respond to. She took a seat next to him.

"Are you also headed to New York?" the man started.

"Yes, I am. I did not see you in line getting tickets for tomorrow's flight," said Alexandra, accidentally disclosing the fact that she was looking for him.

"I am catching an earlier plane. Had to get the first-class tickets. Everything else was booked. I must be home in time. Business calls," he explained.

"What kind of business? What do you do?" Alexandra asked, wondering if it was proper.

"I am an editor of a literary magazine. There is an event I must attend in New York. Can't be late. And what is your occupation?"

Alexandra found it hard to look directly into his eyes. They were dark, sarcastic, and perceptive. She felt they saw right through to her heart. They knew more about the world in general and her, in particular, than she ever would. She must not tell him she loves literature or else he might think that she'll want to use his being an editor.

"I am starting college next week. Haven't decided on my major, though. Undecided. I am interested in math, mostly. Maybe engineering. Not sure yet," she said, involuntarily lowering her eyes to his shoulders. Large shoulders.

"How different we are." The man smiled. "I was just about to get some dinner. Would you like to join me?"

"I? I'd do, would, I don't have money with me, I was just exploring the airport and …"

"I am inviting. It's my pleasure to have your company," interrupted the man.

"Then it's my pleasure to accept," agreed Alexandra.

Alexandra was hungry, and the food smelled awfully good. She had a chicken dish.

"Would you like a glass of wine?"

Sure she would. She had never been involved in such an adventure.

"I believe introductions are in order," the man said. "I am Jonathan."

"My name is Alexandra, but that's too long. Sasha is the Russian short name for Alexandra, but I don't like it. It's a boy's name. Sasha is short for both Alexandra and Alexandr."

"Then can I call you Alexa? The Lovely Alexa?" the man suggested, his eyes sparkling with dare.

"Oh yes! I'd like that!" Immediately, she decided to use this name everywhere from this moment on.

Alexa answered a multitude of Jonathan's questions about her life. He seemed more interested in her than anyone ever was. Yes, she traveled to Russia often. Every summer, with her grandparents. Her grandmother would be returning to New York next month. Alexa had to catch an earlier flight since she was to attend the university next week, and her grandfather accompanied her. Yes, they moved to the United States during Perestroyka, when parents went to work for months without pay. Her parents had good jobs now. She liked New York. She considered it her home now. Her grandparents did not. Her grandmother often expressed guilt over leaving Russia—her country, her homeland.

Jonathan pushed for details. Soon, he appeared to possess her whole life story. However, every time he tried to sway her toward describing her private life, Alexa became shy, confused, and unclear.

"Such a regular traveler, you probably have two sets of boyfriends—the Petersburgers versus New Yorkers. Am I right? Do they know of each other?"

"No, not really," giggled Alexa.

"You are such a tease! They are like two sports teams representing their countries in competition for you. Are you a strict judge? How do you select the winners?"

"I? I don't know. I always feel myself very Russian among Americans and very American among Russians. It's the way they perceive me, I guess."

"That's good; the judge should set herself apart from the rest.

But tell me some rules of the game? Is there a leader in each team?" continued Jonathan. "Are there strategies they work out to score points? I bet each point is worth a kiss! Am I right?"

Alexa giggled a maybe.

"Don't be shy. You can tell me. We are in a neutral zone, and I am not a spy for either of two sides. Do you write them passionate love letters?"

"Sometimes," said Alexa. "To those who score points."

"I knew you are a tease!" exclaimed Jonathan. "I should confess, I first noticed you in St. Petersburg airport. When you were talking on the cell phone. But I never expected we'd get to know each other."

"Me neither," echoed Alexa.

When Jonathan found nothing else to ask, he turned the conversation around. "You do realize that technically we are having dinner in Paris? Have you ever been to Paris?" No, Alexa had not. Well, a few months ago, he spent a few weeks here. One of his friends was involved in the fashion industry, and so Jonathan had tickets for glamorous runway shows closed to the general public. He also attended philharmonic concerts. He loves classical music. Soon, Alexa was lost in the flow of composers and performers she had never heard of. She was dazzled. Amazed. In love.

The dinner neared the end. The plates were empty, but Jonathan still talked, and Alexa listened with her elbows on the table, her head leaning forward. How much she'd like to experience his lips on hers. She practiced looking directly into his eyes without bashfully lowering them onto the table. She did not want to leave the small restaurant. Perhaps she could bring her book and read by Jonathan's side in his waiting room. But soon Jonathan remembered that Alexa was probably missed by her grandfather, and he sent her away with profound goodbyes. Keeping her soft palm in a handshake a few seconds longer than casual, he asked who she was talking to on the cell phone back in St. Petersburg. It was Alexa's grandmother. Jonathan released the girl's hand.

* * *

Could it be over, her adventure? Slowly, Alexa walked back to the large waiting room.

"Where were you so long? We should get something to eat," greeted her grandfather, and Alexa felt she descended back to Earth from the wonderful flight to another world. She couldn't refuse unless she was willing to explain that she already had dinner. She was not willing, and so had to follow her grandfather, listening to his disapproval. She should not have bought that expensive book in the airport. She had plenty of unread Russian books at home. Why did she need to buy an English one? Now they could not have a wholesome dinner, because tomorrow they also needed to get breakfast. They'd have to get something light. An apple pie. For both of them.

Could Alexa leave without seeing Jonathan again? Could she ask him for a kiss? He seemed to like her. Why else would he invite her to dinner and call her Lovely Alexa. She must have his kiss to treasure in the history of her life. Her first real kiss is an important milestone in her timeline. She might never meet another man so amazing, so exceptional. Sure, she liked some boys in high school, even held hands with one once. But she had never felt such defined need for anyone's presence, anyone's closeness, a man's touch.

An elderly American couple from their flight sat at the table next to them. The woman smiled in Alexa's direction.

"Why is she smiling?" asked the grandfather, in Russian. "Tell them this isn't the time to smile. Tell them."

Alexa turned to the couple and translated, "My grandfather said it's too bad we are stuck here, but at least the apple pie is good."

The woman smiled wider, "Are you originally from St. Petersburg? Such a beautiful city. Tell your grandfather that my husband and I just spent two weeks there, but didn't get nearly enough."

To her grandfather Alexa said, "Such are the circumstances. There was nothing anyone could do about our flight being delayed."

"Tell them that such circumstances did not happen back in the old days. All these new government regulations, all these novelties, and here's the result. We are stuck in the airport for the night. And nobody's guilty, nobody's responsible, everyone is smiling."

Alexa translated that a lifetime in St. Petersburg is not enough to fully enjoy it. She asked the couple if they had seen anything in Mariinsky Theater, and received a lengthy admiration of Russian ballet in response. She felt smart and guilty.

Her grandfather pushed the larger pie portion toward Alexa. She chewed and chewed. Sticky apple filling clung to her teeth, sucking out the pleasant taste of wine. On one tooth she was guilty of spending money they now could use. Another tooth ached that she was having the food she didn't want, leaving her grandfather hungry for the night. A painful cavity reminded her of the concealed small, waiting room with comfortable chairs her grandfather could have enjoyed. Sweet crumbs got in-between her teeth, hurting naked gums with desires to kiss a stranger twice her age who said patriotism is stupidity. Alexa chewed and chewed through the pain. A few more moments, and she will never kiss him. She pushed the last bites into her mouth and said she was going to the restroom.

* * *

Jonathan felt heavy with anticipation of night discomfort. His plane did not depart until 4:00 a.m., but his thoughts were already home. At dinner he learned enough of Alexa to lose interest. She was a nice girl. But too passive for his liking. All that talk about parents and grandparents diminished her attractiveness. He'd like her to have interrupted their chat with a sudden, "Have you read Lolita?" or "Are Parisians as liberal in their love affairs as it is rumored?" Alexa was shy, polite, and therefore predictable. It was nice to have had her company, though. When they parted, he honestly wished her all the best in life.

He did not want to fall asleep for the fear of missing the plane. Jonathan took out the only means of staying awake, the WWII book, although he was too tired for it. Either he got too deep into the narrative or into the clouds of sleep, but for a while he lost track of time. Accumulating minutes translated into subtracted years. Something touched his shoulder, ever so lightly. Pleasantly glided from one shoulder to the other. His eyes met Alexa's.

"Hi," she whispered.

"Hi, you," he whispered back, noting the man sleeping a few chairs away. Only the three of them were in the waiting room. Alexa's erotic radiance was back. Her cheeks were flushed. Her eyes glowing.

"Hi," she repeated, "I know we said goodbyes and I hate to bother you, but since we'll never get to see each other again, I, we need to, should, have something to remember this evening by." She lowered her incredible eyes, and Jonathan fancied that she was looking him over. Moments later, Alexa returned her eyes to his and her voice grew stern, "I like you. Could you please kiss me?"

Amazing!

"That is if you want, of course, because, I mean ..." she quickly retracted back into embarrassed chatter.

Jonathan said nothing more. He took her by the waist and sat her beside him. One of his hands caressed her knee. With the other, he pulled her closer. The girl's delicate arm was barely touching his shoulder, her form so tense Jonathan sensed that one careless movement would send her jumping away. He wanted to steady her against his body. His lips touched hers. Then they touched Alexa's cheek and progressed in a series of tender kisses back to her lips, parting them and entering.

It was a good, deep kiss with an apple taste. Jonathan pulled away to look into Alexa's eyes. They were no longer the embarrassed eyes. They were big and wonderful. He touched the plastic of her glasses, the only garment he could take off. But before he removed the lenses between them, Alexa's body stiffened. She stood up.

"Thank you. I should go now. Thank you," she mumbled, and practically ran out.

He did not see himself in the position of trying to stop her. Why did she leave? Because she was a blond teaser. His blond teaser. He desired her. Strongly.

* * *

She did it. Now she had done it. Her first French kiss. Alexa's heart beat loudly in her lips, her cheeks, her fingertips. She felt she had many excited hearts throughout her body. She could still sense his smell, the heaviness of his hand on her knee. This can't be it. She must see him again. Even for a second.

Alexa ran all the way down and up the flights of stairs to the big hall where her grandfather was waiting. When she entered, she tried to slow herself down to look natural, but any efforts for outward calm made her even more explosive within. She dropped on a chair and observed her grandfather's preparations for sleep.

"Is your book adventure over yet?" he suddenly asked in Russian, "You should get some sleep. Tomorrow's a long day."

What did he mean by a book adventure? Did he suspect something? Did he know of everything? "No, I still didn't finish the book. I'll read for a while. I slept on the plane, so I'm too awake," answered Alexa.

Her grandfather did not respond. Soon he was snoring asleep.

Alexa was desperate to find a polite, acceptable reason to see Jonathan again. She had an idea. A goodbye note! She searched her bag for the envelope of pictures. There was one she liked, her grandparents liked. It was taken a week ago, when she visited her friend's house in the village. She posed on the meadow in her short red dress, with flowers woven into her hair. No glasses or makeup. That's how she'd like him to remember her. Sweet and smiling.

Alexa took time to worry over the message she wrote on the back of the photo. Should she give him the means to contact her? No, she must be a grown-up and treat a travel adventure for what it was. She must not be an annoying, clingy little girl. When the note was done, it was still too early. Jonathan might be asleep. She did not want to wake him. Neither did she want to leave her parting gift for him to find when he woke up, for it would eliminate the possibility of looking into his eyes, of saying goodbye one more time.

Her eyelids grew heavier. To keep awake, Alexa took out the WWII book and continued reading. The horrifying details of war reality busied her imagination. How could it be that she went through all school history classes without ever seriously considering the harsh effects of war on the soldiers? She knew about tragedy, about heroism, but the physical actuality always escaped her. Yet the taste of dirt that got into the soldier's mouth when he fell and nearly lost his life might be the sensation he thinks of more often than of political principles. Still, patriotism cannot be stupidity.

At 3:30 a.m., Alexa thought it was too early. At 3:40, she got scared that it was too late. She stood up, looking at her sleeping grandfather, then at the other passengers. It didn't matter what they thought. She was to see Jonathan one last time, and nobody could stop her.

Her heart was racing again. Faster with each step. Down and up the flights of stairs. What if he already left? What if ... The small waiting room was filled with people. The gate to Jonathan's plane was nearby, and boarding was about to take place. He was there. Getting things in order, making his hand-baggage ready. He did not seem pleased to see her.

"Oh, Alexa. I thought you'd be sleeping now," he said dryly.

"I? I didn't want to. So I figured I'd stop by and say goodbye one more time. Here. Don't open this until the takeoff is over." She extended a photograph wrapped in the white leaf from her notebook.

The administrator asked passengers to proceed into the airplane. Jonathan smiled. He was tired and eager to get home. He took Alexa's package, gave her hand a quick shake, and disappeared through the gateway.

Alexa watched as men and women followed Jonathan into the narrow corridor leading toward the plane. They were now his fly-mates, and it made her sad. In a few hours she would have to go through another takeoff herself. She dreaded the takeoff, this unstable transition both drastic and inevitable between the two states of being. The transition from the safe and familiar up to the strange and turbulent. The transition similar to her growing up, only accelerated and condensed into a few minutes.

The present sadness, however, dulled her fears. Losing Jonathan out of sight, Alexa struggled with the first wave of deep regret for not giving him her phone or e-mail. Maybe, just maybe, it was one of those exceptional cases of true love. They could get married and have children as soon as she finished college. She imagined the wonderful evenings they'd have—she'd do her homework, he'd do his editor's work, whatever it was. They'd have dinner together, he'd read a romantic novel to her before sleep, and of course, they'd make love. Why, why did she miss her chance for happiness? She thought about Jonathan before falling asleep every night, for many nights to come, until she met someone, and it no longer mattered. But when she broke up, it mattered again. For a while.

* * *

Jonathan was happily aware of Alexa's gift, waiting in his pocket. The mystery! What could she have given him? As soon as he settled into the comfort of a first-class seat, he felt the folded paper with his hands, and found the photograph edges. A photograph! If she gave him a naked photo of herself and her phone number, he would call her the very next day. What an exceptional girl! His blond teaser! Following Alexa's instructions, Jonathan did not unfold the white paper until a few moments after the takeoff. And then he saw a child in a red dress, bathing in the field of bright flowers.

He turned the picture over and read the message, "It was the most wonderful first kiss I could ever dream of. You kissed my heart, and I will always carry you with me. I kiss you a million times. Please remember me. Alexa."

A growling realization crawled through Jonathan's body and clawed at his mind—just a few hours ago he was burning with passionate desire for a child. He French-kissed a child! Instead of being young, bright, and cunningly dirty, she was young, bright, and innocently sweet. Jonathan was disgusted with himself. So disgusted he felt like ripping up the photo and throwing it away, but he could not. He put it safely into his bag and later into the depths of his writing table drawer, never to be looked at again.

MICHAEL CHEVAL 2007

# *Alice*

Alice stopped taking the subway to work in preference to taxis, even though her house was only a few train stops away in the downtown direction, not out of any physical ailment or a bubble of self-importance but because of condoms. There they were, every day one or two new ones on the train platform in the corner. She would think she should not even be noticing them, or she should regard them as common garbage, no more than an empty can of Coke or a candy wrapper. She would think she should be disgusted at someone's impropriety, someone's amorality and disrespect toward himself, his partner, and the public. But instead, Alice was curious as to what and who and how. And much more than curious, she was very bothered, annoyed, hurt, for she hadn't had a significant other, a soul mate, a partner, a boyfriend, anyone for many years.

Most of her time Alice devoted to work that rewarded her with a successful career, promotions, and salary. Evenings of acute loneliness and distress when her friends were all occupied with their own affairs, Alice treated with expensive spa packages, massages, and haircuts. Theater, opera, even the movies, although she enjoyed them, Alice gave up as they brought more loneliness and distress. She often recalled how, years ago, one of her university friends honestly exclaimed, "How I admire your ability to just take off and go to a performance. I could never go alone." Alice was proud then: she needed no one to take her out to an event she was interested in. Well, years passed. That friend was happily married a long while back, and Alice found herself slowly giving up on events and activities, those beautiful galas that followed symphony orchestra concerts, those strange, independent movie projects, all of them because they always accentuated her single status by an empty chair across her table, an amorous couple seated next to her, an absence of a dance partner, a necessity to go and get her own drink, etc.

Alice was far from invisible. Gala events brought forth winking older gentlemen who asked her to dance and firmly pressed her to their protruding bellies as they talked of glamorous black-tie evenings or fashion events to which they could offer invitations. Alice hurried to escape, always polite and rigid. Why would they think of her that way?

And occasionally, there were charming young men who made her heart fire up with possibility. They were attentive and interesting. Young professionals, like herself, enjoying the night out. During the weeks following the party, Alice waited for them to call and finally called herself just to find them unreachable, unavailable, uninterested. It would slowly come to her that their passionate goodbye looks weren't a desire to see her again but a hope that maybe she'd go home with them that very night.

Friends always tried to set her up with dates too. But enough of staring out the limo window and thinking gloomy thoughts. Alice was almost at the airport now.

* * *

She had not been on vacation for quite some time and decided to pleasure herself with a white limo, first-class tickets from New York, and an expensive hotel suite in LA. But everything appeared at odds with her plans for a divine experience: the limo driver was conspicuously reticent throughout the long drive, and the limited-edition designer glasses that she picked up only a day earlier were too big for her. They kept slipping off every time Alice lowered her head, and twice she caught them in midair.

She endured a few long moments rustling her papers to check the tickets and then communicating with the reluctant driver to address the matter of terminals. Finally, they stopped and she stepped out onto the pavement. Without saying a word, the limo driver helped her with baggage, which was only one small suitcase. He continued displaying, almost theatrically, absolute ignorance of her presence. Alice wondered if she should be giving him tips under such circumstances, and then she did, just because she decided on that in advance. He coughed something in response, which she took for a "thank you." Then, he disappeared inside his vehicle, his displeased countenance unchanged.

Alice bent down to get the suitcase, and her glasses slipped off again. She threw her hands forward, attempting to catch them, but instead, her palm sent them flying down at a greater speed until they hit the pavement edge and jumped right under the back wheel of a departing white limo. There was a crack, and the limo sped out of sight, leaving Alice to contemplate the sharp, sparkling pieces of a tiny tragedy, unknown to anyone but herself.

* * *

Her eyesight was very weak, and contact lenses were packed deep inside the suitcase. Alice found herself instantly transported onto a canvas of colors and blurry shapes, some stationary, others on the move. Unwilling to unpack, she decided she could manage without glasses. But her bravura was lost, and her long heels no longer knocked a sure staccato with each step.

Once inside, Alice asked for directions to find her flight's check-in booth because she had trouble reading the signs. The prospect of waiting was painful as it proffered time to think about the signs that she failed to see. He said she was too intense. What an unpleasant word choice. But according to her friend, that was exactly what he said about her. "She is too intense, too eager. There's this expectancy in her eyes. Like she's a jumping puppy I am responsible to take out for a walk. It's our fourth date, and she just keeps jumping, metaphorically speaking, of course. I don't know, just too intense."

Alice was tired and cynical about men her friends set her up with. However, this one she actually did like. He was easy to speak with and attractive. On their first dinner date, he mentioned an artist he liked. She did not give it much thought, but the next day at work, the artist's name surfaced in her memory, and she searched for him online. There was a ton of biographical information and his paintings were interesting. Alice clicked around until she stumbled upon a small, italicized line about an opening reception for the artist's exhibition scheduled at the end of the week.

Yes, Alice planned to wait until her date called her first, but then they could miss the opening. She was excited; she called him. Before she could tell him about the gallery, Derek said he was busy and promised to call her back in the evening. Alice waited; Derek did not call. Maybe he really was busy. This seemed natural as he held a serious managerial position, and she knew all too well what it meant to be busy at work. He did not call the next day, nor the next. Clearly he was not interested, but there was the gallery opening and really, he was worth taking one more chance. Alice called again on the day of the opening.

Derek sounded polite and very cheerful. He said he could not make it that evening, but it would be wonderful if she went to the gallery and told him all about it when they saw each other next week. Alice did go and did enjoy the reception. On her way home, she felt herself happy in the sweet mix of impressions left by the paintings combined with a pleasant anticipation of next week's date with Derek.

This time he did call and they did go out. Derek listened attentively to Alice's excited account of her trip. The dinner passed by in good cheer and smiles. But then, he failed to call again. By now Alice was burning with desire to see him. Maybe he belonged to the type of men who are fully submerged in their responsibilities at work. That was okay as long as she was the one he came back to in the evenings. In her fantasy she was already Derek's girlfriend, greeting him with a special dinner as he returned from a long, tiresome workday.

Time, the greatest sculptor, shapes and twists the most solid of notions. There was a time when Alice wrinkled her nose and announced that there was no way she would cook or clean for some man. She was a businesswoman, an outgoing woman, and her man should better be prepared to dine out every evening. Now, she fantasized about cooking, about a homemade candlelight dinner with Derek.

She called him again and again, not wishing to play hard-to-get games, believing that she had to do everything possible to make this relationship work.

"Like she's a jumping puppy I am responsible to take out for a walk. I don't know, just too intense." Alice had no idea Derek felt this way. Now, she recalled uncertain, blurry signs lingering in the background of her short-lived relationship. She ignored those shapes, focusing instead on her own bright and clear desires that dominated the picture. She understood now. He wanted a light, flirtatious butterfly of a successful, independent woman. Alice was needy; she was eager. She was thirty-five, and she had not had intimacy for years. She was nervous, frustrated. She really was intense. If only Derek just took a chance with her. If someone wanted her, admired her, kissed her, she would calm down. She would open her wings and be his butterfly.

* * *

There was someone very special, very dear to Alice. She was twenty-three, twenty-four then. But the love must have been too big for her, as it kept slipping off every time she lowered her head. Twice she caught it in midair. Then it slipped off for the third time. She threw her hands forward attempting to catch her love, but instead, her own palm sent it flying away at a greater speed. It disappeared out of sight, leaving Alice to contemplate the sharp, sparkling pieces of a tiny tragedy, unknown to anyone but herself. She never had a boyfriend since then.

* * *

Alice in Wonderland, she thought. She got past the check-in and now walked up and down the hall: stores, signs, people, all dripped into one another. How vulnerable and weak did she feel without her glasses. She'd never been on vacation with a boyfriend. Present situation offered a perfect romantic opportunity. She would hold on to his hand and trust him to lead the way. He'd take her to a store and buy her something: a watch or a ring. Putting the glittering object on, he would kiss her hand and then jokingly forbid her to bring her hand up to her nose. She would feel the present and see its shiny, blurry shape. Of course, Alice would not look at it closely. She would savor the pleasure of his gift for hours before seeing it clearly, when they got to LA.

She would feel the present moment and see its shiny, blurry shape. She would feel it, wear it, and marvel. Years later, she would see the happiness of the present clearly, when she and her husband lay in bed, recalling their first vacation together.

On this note, should she buy something for herself now: a watch or a ring? No, too much trouble without her glasses, too pointless.

Alice recalled a dream from two nights ago. In the dream, she had a ticking clock down below, between her legs. She wondered now whether the clock counted time since her last time or the time left until her next time. Suddenly, it was so important to know the answer, but there was none. Maybe the clock was a time bomb. If she were an artist, she would draw it. No, she would not: the image felt too vulgar for a painting.

* * *

Alice walked down the long, narrow corridor leading toward the airplane. At the plane entrance, she stumbled, dropping her laptop bag and a handbag. A flight attendant prevented her from falling down herself.

"Oh, so sorry."

"Be careful there."

He picked up her belongings and walked her to the seat. Alice could only note that he was shorter than she, had red hair and strong arms. She could not be quite sure about his face. She thought he was smiling.

Her seat was truly comfortable. She took her light jacket off, settled down near the window, and watched as other passengers walked by. First-class seats meant getting onto the plane faster but waiting for it to take off longer. Soon Alice was disappointed to discover that no one sat down next to her. There were only a few passengers in the first-class section, and they sat too far away for her to see clearly. Not that she expected anything different, but still, she maybe hoped for maybe someone.

Before the takeoff, the redheaded flight attendant walked down the aisle, checking that everyone had their seat belts on. He stopped by Alice and asked if he could please place her jacket in the overhead compartment.

"Oh, sure. Of course."

Redhead took her jacket, folded it neatly, and put it away. As he walked on, Alice wondered what his objective was. Her jacket, lying on the empty seat beside her, could not possibly be a bother to anyone.

The engines began to roar, and Alice remembered how her parents always held hands during takeoffs. She glanced at an empty seat, a symbol so cliché and all the more painful for it. She clasped her own hands together and closed her eyes.

* * *

When the seat belt sign was finally off, Alice took her laptop out to make sure it was all right after the fall. She always traveled with her laptop, in case there was some work emergency she needed to address.

Redhead came by, asking passengers what they would like to drink. Her body still remembered where his hands touched it when he caught her. Alice asked for orange juice. The flight attendant filled her glass. Then, he filled another glass with tomato juice, opened the adjacent seat table, and left the glass on it. Before Alice could express her surprise, Redhead moved on down the aisle. Maybe he did not hear her right.

To her great relief, the laptop was fine. She turned the power on and opened Paint. Recently Alice discovered that drawing silly little cartoons was incredibly soothing to her nerves. She realized that they did not look very well and weren't very funny either, but they worked their magic in calming her down when she was upset. The necessity of bringing her face right up to the screen in order to see her drawing was an extra challenge to keep herself occupied.

"She is too intense, too eager. There's this expectancy in her eyes. Like she's a jumping puppy I am responsible to take out for a walk." So the root of the problem was her intense disposition. Okay, she was a puppy demanding to be walked, but that couldn't be all she was.

*"Sometimes I feel there is more to myself than I know about. There is something so tender and beautiful ..."*

* * *

The flight attendant came by to collect her empty glass and the tomato juice that Alice did not touch. Asking about it felt redundant: probably a small misunderstanding. After a short while, he came by again, this time bringing two small bottles of red wine. Alice was busy with her cartoon, and when she raised her head to form a question, Redhead was already turning to walk away. Was this some special first-class routine to bring things she did not ask for? But why then the two bottles? Alice thought about it but drank the wine. First one bottle and then the second.

Soon she was giddy and comfortable. This time, Redhead will not get away from her, she decided. When Alice saw him walking down the aisle, she pretended to be busy with her laptop. When he approached and reached his hands for the empty bottles, she quickly raised her inquisitive eyes to his blurry face.

"May I ask you something?"

"Yes, madam. Would you like anything else?"

"I'd like to know. You do know that I am traveling alone, right?" She waited for him to respond, but he did not. "Why do you keep bringing me two of everything? Twice of everything. Double things. And my jacket too." Alice felt the wine choosing her words but could not do much about it. Redhead still stood there in silence, and she became aware of the wide smile across his face, which made her shiver.

"May I sit down?" he finally asked.

Alice watched Redhead taking a few steps aside, as if to let someone pass through, and then lowering himself to the seat beside her.

"My name's Dave. What's yours?" he asked in a very relaxed, friendly manner. Alice urged herself to calm down. It was probably her eyes playing tricks on her. She couldn't recall having to manage without glasses or lenses for an extended period of time on any earlier occasion. Still, it felt very unnatural to have a flight attendant seated next to her. She could now see freckles all over his face, and they suited him.

"Alice," she answered.

"Alice," he repeated slowly. "Alice, I have a confession to make."

She hoped he would continue speaking without her participation, but Dave held out a long pause that forced Alice to take her turn. "Okay, please tell me what's going on."

"No, no, nothing to worry about. Look at you, so tense. Am I making you nervous? Please, nothing to worry about. Give me your hand." Dave took her hand and held it between his two palms. "Your hand is so cold. Why is your hand so cold?"

This time, no pause could make Alice respond, and after a considerable silence, Dave continued, "I have a friend. A very rich friend. Filthy rich, as they say. Last month he celebrated his thirty-seventh birthday with a grand party. Maybe you read something about it in newspapers, did you? Quite a few celebrities were attending, and this generated some press."

Dave fell silent looking at Alice. His bold familiarity combined with his very physical occupation of her private space made her feel sticky and unpleasant. She wanted to get rid of him, but curiosity urged her to wait a bit longer. "No, I did not read anything about it. I don't read much gossip articles, though."

"That's a pity. He booked a place at Chelsea Piers, especially designated for gala events. Dinner, dessert, dancing. He even had artists there. Those that take no more than five minutes to make a funny cartoon portrait of you. It's amazing to watch them. I don't know how they do it. Are you an artist, by any chance? I saw you working on something there."

"No, not at all. I am into business."

"So I thought," said Dave, and squeezed her hand. Alice decided it was time to take it away from him.

"My friend is very popular with women. They go wild over him," continued Dave. Alice withdrew her hand and pretended to look for something in her handbag.

"He is truly handsome, in a traditional movie star way," said Dave, reclaiming her hand as soon as she put it down on her lap. "There is only one thing that he wishes different in his life. He needs a wife, a home."

"I would imagine there are enough candidates for that position," said Alice, freeing her hand once more, this time pretending to fix her hair.

"Many candidates for sure. Too many. Some of them are openly after the money and the lifestyle, others are secretly after them. Yet most are just not right. It's hard to find the one you'd want to invite into your life." Dave extended his hand onto Alice's lap and covered her hand there. "Into the real private life, not just the image life. He is a very intelligent man. He wants someone who shares his interests. He wants to find his match."

Dave fell into another one of his pauses. Alice imagined him falling gracefully over the edge of his last sentence into a hole of silence. Usually, people stumbled into pauses and went down awkwardly, quickly looking for words to pick themselves up. Dave's fall was more of a smooth slide. He slid down, holding Alice by the hand and pulling her with him. Down, down, down, they descended through the rabbit hole that once led Alice to Wonderland. It was entirely up to her when she wanted to reach the bottom.

"What do I have to do with all this?" Alice asked.

"That's the heart of my story," answered Dave. "Somebody invited a fortune-teller to my friend's birthday party. She said that life has given him much already. Everything went well for him. Even hard work was more of a pleasure than a struggle. She said he would not find happiness with girls seeking his attention. Finding true love might prove to be the most challenging task of his life but also his greatest achievement. 'Start by booking a flight for May eleventh,' she advised him and said no more, although he asked many questions and offered much money for her answers."

"Today is the eleventh of May," noted Alice after a short pause.

"My friend made a show of laughing at the prophecy," continued Dave, "but somewhere in his heart, he must have believed it since he booked a flight to Paris for May eleventh. However, an urgent business matter made it impossible for him to fly today. That's when he called me for the first time in years. He called me and asked for help."

"Wait a second, first time in years? Weren't you just at his birthday party?"

"Yes? Yes, of course! But we barely talked at the party. He was too busy with all the guests. We were very good friends once. Shared a dorm room back in the old college days. But life sent us walking different paths. Every once in a while we get together to catch up on each other's life, but weeks turn to months, months to years. You know how it goes."

Dave paused, and Alice waited patiently for him to continue. She no longer tried getting rid of his hand. Strange as it was to hold hands with a flight attendant, no one else had done it in a very long while.

"He asked me to help him. Even offered me money, but I refused. Only accepted his promise to help me find another job, in case if this little adventure will cost me mine. I gave him my word—he will be seated next to the most beautiful woman on my plane, and she will feel his presence."

Dave gave Alice a long, meaningful look. She felt a man's presence indeed. Must she be responding to the story in general or the compliment in particular?

"Thank you," she said. "Are you sure there aren't any hidden cameras for some TV show?"

"No, of course not. My story is absolutely true. And if I may ask for a personal favor, please don't make complaints about me. I had this job for over five years and would really like to keep it." Now, Dave removed his hand, and Alice felt it as a loss of something she grew attached to.

"Is there anything I am supposed to do?"

"Oh, nothing at all. Just please bear with my strange behavior until we arrive to LA. I should go now, before anyone misses me."

"If anything, you can say I had flight anxiety and needed help," offered Alice as Davc got to his feet.

"Well, thank you, Alice. I did make the right choice."

"What's his name?" she asked.

"Rudolf," answered Dave and walked away up the aisle.

* * *

How bizarre, but what a wonderful story. Two people living their lives, not knowing anything about one another and suffering their individual disappointments. Finally, there is a chance for them to find happiness. But first, there is a test they both must pass, the test of faith.

The tricky fortune-teller is as much help as a hindrance. A sensible, grown man has to believe her and convince his friend to play out this bizarre game. A brokenhearted, desperate woman has to accept her part in the game as well. Maybe this is her chance. Their chance. No more disappointments and misunderstandings. Everything will fall into place and proceed to a happy relationship. If she could never do things in a natural way, the way of her parents and her friends …

*"Daisy, quit fooling around and use your straw properly." … maybe this wild possibility will work out against all odds.*

*"Sorry guys, I am involved in a long-distance relationship*
*With someone big, important, and VERY HOT."*

* * *

Alice put her laptop away when Dave brought dinner. He placed one tray in front of her and another tray in front of Rudolf. Alice thought she saw Dave winking at her, but she was not sure. He walked on to take care of other passengers, and Alice began to unwrap her food.

"Rudolf, will you be eating your cake? May I have it then? You can take my salad. No, I don't eat salad at all. Well, now you know."

Once the dinner was over and Dave collected both trays, sweet fatigue enveloped her body. Alice pushed her chair backward, pulled the blue blanket around herself, and closed her eyes. She imagined she was leaning against Rudolf's shoulder. He would kiss her hair so quietly that his kiss would cross over into the land of dreams and stay with her until she awoke. He would admire her, love her. He would capture her accidentally or purposely disclosed disappointments of the past and lock them inside a history textbook, where they would no longer hurt her heart. She would stop lamenting the lonely years, the dark, empty nights. She would be satisfied and secure.

In winter, they would spend a Saturday at the Met Museum. Then they would catch a two-horse carriage for a ride around Central Park. The darkness, gathering around them, and the snow, falling quietly to the ground, would make it necessary for them to sit closer and to whisper. In summer, they would go to a nude beach. Alice could never go alone and hesitated suggesting it to her friends. She would do it all with Rudolf, all of it.

* * *

Rudolf wouldn't be all about work and business. He would be an art collector. He would show her the meaning of modern-art paintings, those seemingly random circles, squares, and lines that told her no stories. Alice would be a princess giving her suitor a task he must accomplish before marrying her. Yes, Rudolf would want to marry her. She would not have to be like her still unmarried girlfriends, who dreaded bringing up "the subject" they knew would "scare" their boyfriends away. No, Rudolf would truly love Alice and consider marrying her a great happiness. She would agree to marry him only after he taught her about modern art. It does not matter if he sends her to take a class with a world-renowned professor at Harvard or to spend a few months in a cellar with a starving artist. He would open her eyes. No, her eyes were already open, but her vision was so weak. Rudolf would give her glasses and through their lenses, she would reach a higher level of vision, a new awareness of the world. There would be a moment when Alice would experience a sudden, sharp, "Ah," a gasp of perception. After this, she would offer all her gasps to her hero. Rudolf would marry the princess; they would have two children and live happily ever after.

* * *

Alice woke up when Dave touched her shoulder.

"I am so sorry to wake you, but we are almost in LA. Could I please take a picture of you, you know, for Rudolf?" he asked.

"Sure, but oh, my hair must be a mess, can you wait until I ..."

"You are beautiful. Truly beautiful," he interrupted.

Alice looked at the camera, deciding if she should smile or keep a neutral countenance, until Dave snapped the picture, and it was too late to change anything. Then he bent closer to her.

"Would you mind giving Rudolf your e-mail or a phone number so he can contact you in some way?"

Alice was waiting for this question to come up but was still unprepared for it. She hesitated giving him a business card with work information. Instead, she searched the bag for a piece of paper to write down her name and home e-mail. This she gave to Dave, who gazed into her eyes and took a long time letting go of her hand.

When the airplane landed, she gathered her belongings and joined the stream of passengers. At the exit, she exchanged light goodbye nods with Dave. As she walked away, Alice wondered if she should turn around and look at him once more, but then decided against it. It was hard enough to see where she was going.

* * *

Vacation week flew by quickly without much action. Alice made one shopping trip, visited a museum, and spent an evening at a nightclub. She imagined herself a beautiful, slim lady running down the beach at the same early hour each morning. But after the first such morning, she excused herself from the exercise, thinking that she had to wake up early for work and was allowed some sleep on vacation.

There was one handsome man. Alice noticed him in a restaurant at breakfast. A cup of coffee grew cold on his table while he read a book. The next morning she saw him again. On the third day, Alice decided she would speak to him; perhaps ask him what he was reading. But she did not see him again, even though she made it her business to arrive at the restaurant earlier and sit there for longer every day until the end of her stay.

The man's handsome features, his broad shoulders, his thick heap of black hair became the physical image of Rudolf, the perfect man. Alice fantasized about him throughout the week, staying away from Internet cafes in fear of getting or not getting his letter.

* * *

Alice arrived home late at night. She dropped her bags by the door and rushed to the computer without even taking her jacket off. It was there: "Dear, Beautiful Alice" read the subject.

> Hello, my beautiful Alice. It was a great pleasure meeting you. Am I correct to assume you were on a business trip to LA? Your husband must be very dumb letting you go alone. I have a lot of experience accompanying such wonderful ladies as you are. For a very reasonable price, I will play any game you like and give you the time of your life. I will never intervene with your schedule but will be at your service whenever you'd want me around.
>
> I believe we have a special connection, a special understanding between us. Don't hesitate to call me or write me any time, day or night. (My phone: xxx-xxxx)
>
> Your Loving Dave.

Alice sat and looked at the screen. Disappointed. Tired. Mostly she was tired. Only five hours were left until she would have to wake up and go to work. On the bright side, she had a massage appointment she scheduled before going on vacation. This was something her friend recommended as a divine experience.

The mouse moved to delete Dave's e-mail but hit reply

instead.

> Hello, my loving stranger. There is something I want to ask you. I have a secret fantasy I can never share with my husband. Would you ever make love to me on a subway station at night and leave the condoms lying on the platform so I can look at them on my way to work in the morning?
>
> Alice

The reply she received the next evening was positive, dirty, and unforgettable. Alice deleted both e-mails.

Why were her stories always fiction? Wasn't there a man who would admire her strength and love her weakness? Alice was naïve, imaginative, insecure. Her vision was very poor, but could no man see it as a perfect romantic opportunity? Would no one take her by the hand and lead her through life, turning the blurry world into a fairy tale where anything is possible, even love. In turn, she will provide her hero with wonderful words, settings, and action. May eleven years of loneliness be enough. May her next one be right, be true, be with her.

MICHAEL CHEVAL
2007

# *Charmer's Birthday*

Charmer walks through the forest. Tall and short, he fits into nests, flowers, berries, beehives, hills, and hollows. Light and heavy, he rests on petals and falls as grand barks of ancient trees. Merry and belligerent, he is welcome at all festivals and all battles. Sweet, roaring, and whispering, he speaks with the birds, the bears, the butterflies. His words belong to the language of the woods. His voice is a continuous mixture of forest sounds. He suffers his insomnia with wide, round, yellow of owl's eyes or falls asleep in a closing flower to wake up sparkling with the morning dew. Familiar and mercurial, famous and unremarkable, he is admired, loved, feared, and ignored by forest dwellers.

Without the forest, Charmer would cease to exist, as he would no longer be seen, heard, smelled, touched, or tasted. His identity is part of the forest, and the only proof of his identity, the only traces of his existence, are the sequences of forest sights, noises, smells, textures, and tastes that he chooses to record by living through them.

Once upon a time, a young girl of six or seven came to the forest with her parents to gather mushrooms. She ran from one tree to another as fast as she could, but her basket remained almost empty. Her father offered to share his mushrooms, but the girl refused, as it was not the mushroom she wanted but the joy of discovery. Her mother found a meadow full of little foxes, the small yellow mushrooms, and called the girl over to pick them. Delighted with the task, as it was always a pleasure to gather little foxes, the girl got right on her hands and knees, something her parents told her not to do because grass stains were hard to wash off and for a more serious fear of snakes and other biting creatures. The girl got right on her hands and knees, close to the smell of grass, the earth, and the mushrooms. She played and she gathered until she looked up to see the White. The White was a mushroom king of the forest. It was a special honor to find one. Whenever a grown-up came back to the village with a large basket full of Whites, everyone commented on his wonderful work because besides being suitable for various cooking purposes, these mushrooms had a certain charm of aesthetic beauty.

The girl looked at her White as if it were a treasure chest full of gold coins from the picture in her fairy-tale book. She spent weeks obsessed with finding treasure, drawing maps, and drawing friends into wild and brave plans for adventure. At this instant, the White mushroom was precious enough to be considered a treasure. The girl looked around. She could hear her parents nearby but could not see them.

The White was perfect: not fully-grown but large enough and very solid. The girl could almost hear the crisp sound that its leg would make when she cut it with her knife. Still on her hands and knees, she crawled closer to the mushroom.

Meanwhile, Charmer decided to look his forest over from the top of a tall pine. For a considerably long time, he swung on grass edges waiting for a bird to come down and offer him a free lift. But no birds were in sight, and irritated Charmer saddled a ladybug, hoping she would carry him up to the low tree branches from where, leaf-by-leaf, he could climb up himself. The clumsy ladybug rose heavily into the air, heading toward the young birch, and landed on a weak leaf that snapped off the branch. Charmer whispered down with the leaf and the ladybug onto the White's hat.

All of a sudden, the girl saw more than a single mushroom. She saw the grass tightly hugging its leg and the young birch throwing leaf shadows on its hat. The birch seemed to tower over the White, but it was as much a child as a chubby mushroom … as much a child as the girl was. The sunny meadow was a playground and the forest children smiled at her. Ladybug ran off the birch leaf onto the White's hat. The leaf lost its balance and fell to the ground just in time when the ladybug reached the hat's middle and flew off.

Mesmerized, the girl looked on, and Charmer, always eager to prove his existence to a willing observer, disclosed his identity, the compositions of forest senses recorded by his life. The White mushroom took on qualities beyond its value of a treasure chest. The girl could not cut its leg no matter how badly she wanted to fill her basket. Slowly she got up from her knees and gave the mushroom under the birch one last look, capturing the picture that would remain with her, always clear and readily available for viewing.

The girl ran to her parents, and it was on their way back to the village that the agony of a lost opportunity caught up with her. She mumbled about the mushroom she found, but when her mother asked why the girl did not get it, she was unable to explain. There were no words to express the overflowing excitement over the discovery, over the anguish at not collecting the treasure, over the knowledge of undisturbed beauty that remained safely inside the forest forever, recorded by Charmer's powers and now her own.

Back home she wrote a story about a girl named Lisa who was lost in the forest. Extremely anxious and equally excited, she read it to her parents, who admired the story and saved it among the many others that were to follow.

* * *

## Forest Farces

Once upon a time, there lived a girl named Lisa. She was kind, polite, and beautiful. She lived in a big, beautiful house with her mother and father. They had everything, but Lisa always dreamed about adventures and so her home seemed boring and gloomy. When Lisa could stand it no longer, she left her house to look for adventures.

For a long time she walked across the city but then entered the forest and got lost. For a long time Lisa walked through the forest, yelling and calling, but all was in vain. Then she sat down and remembered her home. At this time, she could be finishing her supper and heading for bed. Ah, how wonderful it would be. Lisa looked around, and feeling how lonely and helpless she was, she started crying.

Dark night fell around her. Suddenly, Lisa saw flickering lights and heard someone's gentle voice. She held her breath and listened to a wonderful song.

We are the spirits of the trees;
The trees are our homes.
Our horses are the buzzing bees
And mushrooms are our thrones.

Lisa was very afraid, but hunger and tiredness overcame her fear, and she began walking toward the flickering lights. When she came near them, Lisa saw little funny fellows.

"Who are you?" she asked them.

"We are forest Farces," one fellow answered. "We like playing tricks with those who enter our kingdom at night."

"We flicker our lights and lure people deeper into our forest," continued the second fellow.

"We set traps on their path, so they stumble," continued the third.

"We make leaves look like treasure, and when they come near we jump out and scare them," continued the fourth.

"But we are good spirits. We don't harm anyone. We just play and then we show them the way back home," explained the first fellow.

"Will you scare me, too?" asked Lisa.

"No, we would not scare you. You are one of us. Only you happen to be a girl. Come play with us."

Lisa followed the Farces into the wonderful meadow. There were many mushrooms, and Farces jumped from one to another, dancing and playing and laughing. Little colorful balls flying among the Farces lit the meadow with mysterious, magical light. Farces caught them and threw them at each other, playing a strange game Lisa did not know.

On the dark, far edge of the meadow, the White mushroom grew under the birch. Greenish Charmer with a spider web for his beard looked onto the Festival of Farces. Lisa wanted to ask who he was, but she was too busy dancing and singing with the spirits.

"We like you. Stay with us," said one fellow.

"We will give you butterfly wings and you will fly," continued the second.

"We will crown you and you will never have to do homework or wash the dishes," continued the third.

"All we ever do is play wonderful games," continued the fourth.

"And we help those who love the forest," explained the first fellow.

Lisa always admired beautiful butterflies and wanted to learn to fly.

"Okay, I will stay with you. What do I have to do?" she asked.

"All you have to do is taste our wild raspberry jam," answered Farces and brought out a green glass made of leaves and adorned with flowers.

Lisa took the glass in her hands, when suddenly, Charmer jumped off the White mushroom and ran toward her. He knocked the green glass out of Lisa's hands with his walking stick made of a long, thin tree branch.

"Not the time now," he said. "You must go home, go to school, and develop your character before playing Farce games."

Farces quieted down because they had to obey Charmer. Lisa remembered about home and asked Farces to show her the way. They gave her a large basket full of red raspberries and guided her out of the forest.

Lisa came home only by the morning. Her mother and father opened the door together. As soon as Lisa entered the house, she asked her parents to forgive her. She promised that she would never run away again.

Since then her home seemed merry and happy to Lisa.

But I would not advise you, my dear young readers, to run away from home. Forest Farces might not be there to help you find the way back.

* * *

## Thoughts for Comfort

Those days I remembered—
when I was a child and believed
the world was full of unconquered forests and wild beasts.
Those days I remembered
when the tour guide at the National Park talked
about the marked and counted with labels on their bodies.
For a moment I wanted to go back, back to that green world
where the world seemed.

We live in an anthill
that was once only a small element of the great forest.
Now there are but a few trees
with countless tiny bodies swarming everywhere in-between.
Hardworking ants,
black ants,
ants with wings,
ants handling loads bigger than their sizes,
brown ants,
ants carrying white eggs.
Ants, ants, ants—
like a dot dot dot typed all over the page,
as suffocating as particles of air that make my dad's office

smell of cigarettes,
houses patterned as roots of fur on my cat's tail,
as patterned as pixels on a screen image.

Thoughts of overpopulation
brought by accidentally read newspaper articles, brushed
aside—
it doesn't concern my generation,
the children of the children of my children will figure
something out.
I'll just forget myself in books—millions of them out there.
Is it possible to read every book that I think I should read?
I must visit the zoo
and look at the marked and counted representatives of each
species.

If the book I write doesn't get labeled and cared for,
I'll believe it is happy in a wild, green world.

* * *

Her glossy white shoes stepped into the garden green, and Alice walked by the row of uniformed waiters who held out trays with sparkling wine. Wearing these shoes for the first time, Alice was not sure if she would make it through the evening on such high heels. They looked beautiful on her feet, though. When she noticed them at the store, as she shopped for a new party dress, she knew she had to wear them. The physical comfort was far less important than their perfect fit with her fantasy of imitated White mushrooms in a forest she fancied out of a small garden locked in the middle of the busy New York.

Perhaps this dismissal of reality was too bold, because the party was just beginning and her feet hurt already. Maybe it was due to the blisters left by the other shoes Alice wore earlier. Whites covered her bloody blisters from visibility but also squeezed them tight with each step.

Alice picked up a glass of sparkling wine from a tray held by a smiling young man. Since Whites precluded the pleasure of walking about, she planted herself under the tree beside a small fountain. Whether she liked it or not, Whites, true to their mushroom character, preferred to have their long heels rooted to the ground as they waited for others to approach.

Alice watched the arriving guests: couples, groups of friends, not too many singles. Her thoughts slowly wandered away to bring back a cloud of memory that rained an interesting experience onto her. Next to a fountain under a tree, Alice stood on her mushroom feet in a garden-forest while the invisible rain showered her with fresh drops of moments past.

* * *

Years ago, she was traveling abroad with a university program over the summer. One day, tired of dark jazz bars and loud night clubs to which the majority of her newly made friends gravitated at evening hours, Alice decided to take off alone to a casino located inside a grand hotel plaza that towered over the city. Quickly losing the fifty dollars she allocated for the colorful spinning machines, each one tempting with new possibility, Alice walked across the hall to the stores that stretched in a long line parallel to the casino. Expensive designer bags, dresses, shoes, hats, glasses were as tempting as the possibility of winning a million. Alice dealt with this enticement in the same fashion: by allowing herself to buy a hairpin in the form of a rose and nothing more. In terms of proportions, her purchase was very extravagant, since getting a hairpin for the price she paid was equivalent to buying a designer handbag, a larger object at a larger price. The hairpin was, however, affordable, and Alice wanted to take home at least a small petal from the glamorous city flower, the hotel plaza.

Already getting tired, Alice walked to what she thought was the exit. Instead, the hallway, with stores on one side and the casino on the other, was only a corridor leading into another grand, wide hall. Stepping inside, she was caught off guard by the unexpected range of effects instantly activating her sight, hearing, and smell simultaneously. The black-tiled floor beneath her feet reflected the chandeliers, making Alice feel as if she were about to fall through the black waters. Raising her eyes to look at the chandeliers, she was struck midway by the far wall where the light show was dancing to the sound of classical orchestra melody. Sweet smell of flowers, growing in each corner, hypnotized Alice. She stood motionless for a full minute, or maybe a few minutes, looking down, looking up, listening, and breathing. It was so exciting to take that first step forward, half expecting to fall through the tiles. It was so hard to tear eyes away from the light show on the wall. Alice wanted to get closer to the flowers, to stretch her neck and see the end, or rather the beginning of the chandeliers.

She wondered why there were so few people around. The casino was relatively busy with players, but the stores stood empty, and now she was the only one enjoying the magnificent hall. There should be enough guests to secure sufficient profit for supporting such a place. Where were they?

Alice headed across the black-tiled floor toward the opening and walked out of the gloomy magic into the bright hotel lobby. It was embellished with jewelry showcases and large vases full of hypnotizing flowers. Beside the elevators, Alice noted a few sculptures of embracing, entwining forms that spoke to her other sense, the touch. It would be so natural, so pleasing to take an elevator up to the room and entwine with the lover.

Finishing her circle around the lobby, Alice returned to the magnificent hall. Opposite the light-show wall, black tile stairs rose high up toward the chandeliers. Alice thought of them as glamour stairs. Slowly, she ascended, considering each step. Where would she end up if the black tiles were to become as liquid as they appeared? Would chandelier reflections guide her through the dark labyrinth or charm her deeper into the nameless depths? What was it like to be a mermaid of the magnificent hall? Would she be the first captive or just another one?

Somewhat surprised to find herself still above the surface, Alice stood before a restaurant entrance. It was empty but the tables were set. Smelling meat and pastries, she remembered her sense of taste and asked the smiling young woman at the counter if there were tables still available. The woman nodded her head eagerly and entered Alice's first and last name into the computer for reservation. She said the restaurant would be open in twenty minutes.

Alice went outside and down the stairs to wander around. Who was the genius that designed this place? Every new object coming into view, be it a vase, a sculpture, a chandelier, every new scent flowing from long-stemmed flowers, every new melody accompanying the continuous light show, all of them were waves of pleasure rolling leisurely one after another across the calm waters. Every sense was considered and fully addressed. But how did this masterpiece, this manmade city flower, compare with the natural forest beauty? It couldn't be compared and it shouldn't be. It was part of the forest. It was a human dwelling, much like that of ants, only grown out of proportion.

Alice came back to the restaurant and was seated by a welcoming waitress. The classical music from the hall flowed across the room, and she could see the light-show wall on her left. On her right, a wall-sized window encircled the restaurant. Her table was in the middle of the room, but she was alone and no one obstructed the overwhelming view of the river and the city that lay behind it. City lights reflected in the dark river waters. Ah, this is where the designer got the idea for the black-tile waters reflecting chandelier lights. Perfect. Just so perfect.

Examining her menu, Alice was relieved to see that prices were similar to an upscale New York restaurant, but nothing impossible as she feared it might be. She had continuous internships throughout the school year that paid well and afforded occasional fits of her fancy.

Looking out the window on her right, watching the light show on her left, Alice was not sure just when the table in front of her became occupied by a man and a woman. She could only see the man's broad back, but the woman facing him, and Alice as well, was so painfully familiar. Alice had seen her pictures, watched her interviews, read her books. Could this really be her? Impossible.

For the next hour and a half, Alice considered going up to the woman and asking her for an autograph and maybe even a photo with her. Alice always carried a digital camera in her bag as most other students from her group did. What incredible luck to have a camera, a pen, a paper, and a celebrity seated in the empty restaurant right in front of her. Alice did not even have to twist her neck to see the woman. Yet something held her back.

The couple ate in silence except for a few exchanged words that Alice could not hear. She could sense the comfortable familiarity between them, one that did not require much talking. Maybe this is what held her back, the distaste for distraction, for annoyance she did not want to see on their faces. Once, the woman raised her eyes to look Alice over and then went back to the privacy of her dinner. That's it, the privacy. Alice had too much respect for privacy and for beauty to upset their balance.

The dinner was excellent. A friendly waitress made conversation, asking Alice where she was from and where her group was headed to next. How easy it would be to get up and take a few steps toward the woman's table. What if Alice was wrong? Pictures could be very misleading sometimes. It would be very awkward if she approached the woman to find out she was not the one Alice thought her to be. That's it, the embarrassment. Alice had too much fear of embarrassing herself.

A witch, a beautiful witch, blond witch, that is a beautiful White Witch—that's how Alice would describe her. Of course, this description was largely dictated by the woman's own books, but her writing was so suitable with her appearance. Alice loved her books. It must have taken years before the Ministry of Magic allowed the White Witch to exercise her charms in the Muggle world.

Finally, the waitress brought the couple their check, and it was the White Witch who paid for dinner. The man and the woman got up from the table and walked leisurely out of the restaurant. Alice emptied her plate, waited for her check, and then descended the glamour stairs. Giving the magnificent hall one parting look, she left the grand plaza.

Oh, the agony of lost opportunity! Alice crossed the river bridge heading toward the hotel where she was staying with her group. Maybe the couple would not have minded to spare a second for an autograph. Maybe they would have welcomed it as a short distraction from the monotony of a lengthy dinner. Maybe the White Witch would have been happy to make a short conversation with an admiring fan. In her notebook, in her camera, Alice would have a treasure to show her friends from the group, her friends back home, her parents. It would be something to show her kids, when she has them, who would surely read White Witch's books and watch the movies. But she, Alice, lost the opportunity because she was afraid of making an embarrassing mistake, because of her vague speculations on beauty and privacy. Yet she did not feel empty handed. Rather, she was empty-handed but not empty-hearted, not empty-minded.

This was the last evening her group spent in the city. They were to get on a plane in the afternoon for a new destination. The group's coordinator sat next to Alice at breakfast and asked if she had enjoyed her stay. Hesitantly, Alice told of her encounter with the White Witch. The coordinator smiled, nodded, and changed the subject. She did not believe Alice, seeing her as a shy, quiet student who tried getting some attention. Alice refrained from communicating the story to her roommate or anyone else.

* * *

Sweet was the smell of wild raspberries, but after three days, it became so familiar that Charmer ignored it. He was hiding inside the red ripe berry from the incessant rain. This was no kind summer rain, but one with acidic drops that pinched anything they fell upon. Such rain could only result from excessive, unrestrained bitterness released by one of the forest creatures. Charmer hoped the rain would stop without his involvement, but he was tired of sleeping, and his arms and legs became entangled in his own white web beard. Besides, allowing the rain to continue compromised forest health. The usual remedy to restore general happiness was to get rid of the disturber, be it a bird whose nest was destroyed or a weak animal crying from hunger. Lazily, Charmer climbed out of the berry, now big and heavy with water. Immediately, he wished he could go back and hide from the burning pinches of acidic raindrops. But instead, Charmer smoothed out his white web beard and went in search of the culprit.

* * *

The man approached Alice with two glasses of wine and offered one in exchange for her empty glass. Then he turned away, looking for a place to put the empty glass on. Alice wondered what mushrooms must feel when the gatherers approach them: excitement for being discovered or fear for being noticed.

The man came back and raised his glass in salutation.

"Vlad," he said.

"Lisa," she answered, raising her glass likewise.

They both took time for slow, small sips of wine. The invisible raindrops still falling around Alice got inside their glasses and dived into the wine, making pleasant, peculiar water sounds before dissolving within a bubbly liquid. Then Alice reconsidered.

"Actually, no, it's Alice. Lisa is an alter ego, a onetime accidental invention that grew and developed over the years. Sorry."

"No, I am sorry for interrupting. You looked so deep in thought, staring inside that empty glass. What were you thinking about?"

"Believe me, you do not want to know."

"Of course, I do."

"It's silly."

"All the better. Everyone else is doing a pretty good job being smart about the paintings."

"Do you plan on buying something once the auction starts?"

"I doubt it. I don't acquire art. It's enough that I have to analyze it."

"So you want to hear my In Vino Veritas?"

"Of course."

"I just finished reading J.D. Salinger's short stories. About the Glass family, you know?"

"Of course."

"You know why they are Glass? Glass is so sharp, solid, defined, and clear. And transparent. You can look in from the outside, you can look out from the inside, but there is always a shadow, a lingering ghost of your own self reflecting from the glass and staring back at you. That's what most, if not all, characters do; they have their personalities and their lives, but they always reflect the writer. Even if this is not evident at first, just turn the glass another way, shine the light at a different angle, and there would be the writer looking back at you. So I imagined Salinger, looking out of his window at home or maybe into the store from the street, when he saw a familiar reflection lingering among the contents that lay on the other side, grouped together within the window frame. Objects, events, settings are grouped inside the window frame like in a painting or a story or a musical composition, while the glass, the character, allows us to see those objects, events, and settings through him or herself, inevitably enclosing the writer's reflection inside the mix of all the rest."

Alice took a few sips of wine and continued, "This writer's reflection may be the soul of the work. Maybe the story lives only when the writer shares his or her soul with it."

"Hmm. It's some special glass you had there. But you overlooked the most important detail. A true masterpiece will have the reader see his own reflection once he looks inside the work. It is much trickier to craft a glass out of your character than to paint a self-portrait, however beautiful it might be. Only the glass will reflect the writer for the writer and the reader for the reader."

"Good point. I didn't think of that." Alice assessed Vlad's appearance for the first time. He was dangerously black-haired. Every man she had ever liked since high school had black hair. Does the mushroom have only two choices: to be picked and destroyed in the kitchen or to be overlooked and abandoned to its own solitary demise? She didn't destroy her White mushroom, but nevertheless she kept it. This happened so rarely in life.

After some shared silence and exchanged glances, Vlad tried a new topic.

"What brings you to the auction today?"

"The party, the paintings, the good weather." The wall of invisible rain continued showering Alice. It was surprising that Vlad had even noticed her behind this wall in the first place. Now he stood right beside her, his black hair already wet from her rain.

"What do you do?" asked Vlad.

"You mean my profession?"

"Right. I am almost afraid to hear you answer."

"You should be. I do business. Wealth management."

"You like it?"

"You had to ask. I am good at it. We had a performance evaluation last week, and my manager said I always come up with unusual solutions. I liked that."

"But do you like what you do?"

"Very much so. It's just that I've been thinking a lot recently. Perhaps if I'd had a different job, I wouldn't have been so single for so many years. I might have been a model."

"A model?"

"When I was in my first year of college, I got picked off the street to take modeling classes in midtown. They taught us the walk, the turns, little tricks to take our jackets off gracefully as we turned, and made sure we dropped our hands to our sides when we walked away because elbows do not look good on camera. We were taught to walk the glamour walk, as if we were queens of the world. And the surprising thing was: it worked. It worked so unbelievably well. I just began using makeup. I made sure I came to class wearing something trendy. And I practiced my glamour walk. Men stared at me, yelled and whistled across the street, asked for phone numbers. I was amazed. Once, a man ran out of a hotel restaurant and sprinted down two blocks to catch up with me. And he wasn't some strange, weird guy; at least he didn't look like that. He saw me from the window and just ran out."

"What happened then?"

"Well, he said he was in New York for a few days on business and would really like it if I showed him around. I told him I was a model, which made him even more excited. Finally, I gave a wrong phone number and left. I was just out of high school, and having a fling with a middle-aged business-suited man wasn't something I even thought about. I believe he was good-looking, though. These things don't happen anymore."

"So why didn't you go on with modeling?"

"Got sucked up into college life. Lectures, friends, competing for higher grades. Studying for tests instead of taking an extra shower, doing homework instead of polishing nails, sleeping on the train instead of flirting. There was a specific reason, though. Our regular teacher got sick and the substitute was a real working model. She looked like she stepped off the magazine page. Tall, fashionably dressed, impossibly skinny. She made it her business to tell us all about her modeling experience. Everyone loved her stories, except for me. She said that once we are in Paris, we should be prepared to carry large bags of clothes and personal makeup supplies as we run from one show or casting event to another. Once she missed a casting call for an underwear commercial. She was very upset, but two weeks later, those models who went got diagnosed with some sort of venereal disease because they all had to try on the same underwear one after the other, and apparently, someone ahead of them was infectious. She also told us we must not take rejections personally, as every designer is looking for a particular body type to bring out his vision. Then I thought to myself that running around the city might be fun when I am twenty, but that's not what I imagined for my thirties. I didn't want indifferent men to look me over and decide that my hips are too wide or my breasts are too small. I didn't want my life to depend on their decisions. I didn't want to run around Paris unable to get a taxi. But most of all, I didn't want to risk my health for a chance to be in a commercial. I didn't want to live my life constantly faced with difficult decisions, always compromising, always worrying. So I finished the course, but never went to auditions that were especially set up for us. I just decided it wasn't for me. I'd much rather catwalk through New York streets."

"And now you regret your decision?"

"Yes and no. As I said, if I was a model, I wouldn't be single."

"What kinds of men interest you?"

Alice gulped down the last of her wine and imagined the gigantic raindrops immediately filling her glass up to its brim and spilling out. She watched Vlad drinking from his glass as well and wondered if he could taste her raindrops diluting his wine. She wondered what he thought of her flavor.

"Really, tell me what men do you like," persisted Vlad.

Alice knew he wanted to lighten up the conversation. He was looking for sexy, sweet one-liners, which weren't her strong point. It would take a novel to explain what kind of men she liked.

"I don't know anymore. I really don't know. I am thirty-five, and I've been single for eleven years. I don't know what I like. Maybe nothing."

"Have you tried your glamour walk anytime recently?"

"No. I tend to deeply concentrate on whatever it is that interests me at the moment, and everything else slips my mind. Once, when I was just out of college and began working, I walked through midtown thinking about the meeting I had attended. A man approached me. Instinctively I shook my head and kept on going. Only some ten steps later I realized the man had asked me if I wanted to take part in a popular show they were filming. I turned around just to see him already talking to another young woman who looked a bit similar to me. Tall and blondish, she was smiling, almost jumping with excitement as they walked away together. I was left to my solitary evening of watching a movie, dining, and going home. I must really be asked a few times before I can say yes. I cannot grab a fleeting opportunity. Not in personal life. Work is different."

"Maybe you should try concentrating on love for a change."

"I've done that, once. It's very painful to concentrate on someone while you always slip his mind as he concentrates on something else."

"You mean someone else, right?"

"Not necessarily. If he is too busy building his career and sees me as a pleasant distraction to enjoy whenever he happens to have a free evening, it is little better than someone else. It was many years ago, though. Does not matter now."

Vlad looked away. Alice decided she did not care what he thought about her. She had so many easygoing party conversations. They led to nothing or worse, to heartaches. It didn't matter if Vlad thought she was raving the effusive anguish of an embittered old maid.

She had to be honest for once, and it was better to pour her heart out onto the stranger who would wince with displeasure at her acidic raindrops and disappear, eliminating the necessity to be embarrassed or apologetic afterward.

"Too late now. Years passed. I've gained weight. No, don't interrupt me. I know I am not fat, but no model, either. No more glamour for me. No more Prince Charming."

"Sounds like there never was a Prince Charming."

"There was expectation at first, anticipation later, and hope afterward."

"Modeling isn't the only option. You could act. Sign up to be a movie extra or try out for theater. See how that goes."

"I have no real interest in acting. I'd like it much better to own a theater."

"Is that what you'd really like to do?"

"I think I'd do a good job with all my managerial and finance experience."

"I asked if that's what you'd really like to do."

"I'd rather write." Alice pronounced this very quietly, surprised at the difficulty of it.

"Then get a boyfriend and write."

"But I really enjoy my work. It took so many years to get to where I am now."

"Then keep your job, get a boyfriend, and write. These don't have to exclude one another."

Alice looked down at her White mushroom shoes. Her feet were in pain and she kept lifting them up interchangeably throughout the conversation, but it did not help much. Suddenly, she wanted to go home. Immediately.

"I think I will go now. Thank you for listening," she said.

"But the auction did not even start. You did not even hear the dashing speech I prepared."

"You will be speaking?"

"Yes, introducing the art collection that will be auctioned."

"That's great, but I should go. I can't bear being in my shoes a minute longer."

"Then step out of them. Take them off."

"Right here? No."

"Come on, take them off."

"No. My feet are all in blisters from the other shoes."

"I've already seen your blisters. Take them off now."

They stood under the tree a little off the paved road that ran through the garden. Alice held on to Vlad's hand as she stood on one foot, taking the shoe off the other. Then she switched and took off the second shoe. The grass felt so refreshing to her bare skin. The rain clouds finally parted, allowing the sun to shine. Next to a fountain under a tree, Alice stood in a garden-forest with her wet dress clinging tightly to her skin and exposing her body, each curve highlighted by the beams of sunlight streaming from her eyes.

"I have to go give my speech. Wait for me, butterfly," said Vlad.

Alice nodded.

* * *

**ButteRRRfly**

One called me a butteRRRfly.

My mascaRRRa-black eyelashes flapped,

spRRRinkling scaRRRlet fliRRRtations

to illuminate blond cuRRRly locks

that twiRRRl down spaRRRkling

fRRRom the miRRRRRRoRRR-like paRRRticles

on my bRRRave-RRRed dRRRess

that baRRRely coveRRRs

my secRRRetly RRRunning shiveRRRs

foRRRming neaRRR the staRRRRRRy necklace

and following undeRRRgRRRound RRRoads

beneath the bRRRave-RRRed dRRRess,

twiRRRling down like cuRRRly locks

foRRRcing mascaRRRa black eyelashes to flap

and RRRuby lips to paRRRt

foRRR a peRRRfect "PuRRRRRRRRR"

befoRRRe getting scaRRRed and flying off.

* * *

Vlad meant to come back, but a few steps away from Alice he felt such great relief that he decided to leave her be. He watched her across the garden as he waited to begin his speech.

Charmer, all wet from the biting rain, looked across the meadow. There he saw the cause, the source of acidity, the butterfly, hiding under the White mushroom. He did not care for a wounded insect, but he noticed that flowers were bending their heads toward her and ladybugs were gathering around to listen. The butterfly told them stories about her misfortunes. Only three days ago, she was enjoying the morning sun and fluttering across the meadow from one flower to another until she saw the perfect flower, the brightest, the sweetest. It was one of those rare moments when the object of strongest desire was within her reach, fully accessible, openly inviting. The butterfly hurried toward the flower but something obstructed her way. She could not fly ahead; she could not turn back. She was stuck in a web, looking onto the flower, her desires teased, her taste unsatisfied, her goal impossible. Soft black paws examined her wings. Sharp, sudden pain pierced her body. Then there was a blow—a young girl of six or seven ran through the meadow toward the White mushroom and tore the web without even noticing. The butterfly fell to the ground. She could walk, but her wings were tied together with sticky web strings and would not open.

* * *

Alice looked on toward the podium constructed in the middle of the garden. Vlad talked, but the meaning of his words melted into the sound of his voice and dissolved inside his Cheshire Cat smile. Alice felt something change, something come alive under her dress. Charmer's warm breath dissolved the web strings, freed the butterfly wings, tickled Alice's thighs, and bid her to fly. By the end of the auction, Alice felt she was floating in the air. She did not even notice a large, heavy bird that landed on the meadow and spotted easy prey beside the White mushroom.

"I think I'd like this piece of artwork," a loud, hoarse voice sounded near Alice. She turned around to find a heavily mustached man fixating his drunken eyes on her.

"How much for her?" he asked, addressing people who turned their heads, curious to see what was happening.

"How much for you?" he asked Alice, taking a few steps closer, barely holding his balance.

"How about twenty-five thousand and you are mine? No? How about fifty thousand?" he yelled out, mimicking the auctioneer's accent.

Now all heads in the garden were turned in their direction.

"Rogozhin offered twice as much for Nastasya Filippovna," answered Alice, her voice stern but not without a note of fear. It was the first thing that came to mind and formed a simple union of mathematics and literature.

The man just stared at her, confused. Alice winced from the smell reeking from his drunken breath and his black suit, which was apparently soaked in alcohol.

"Haven't you read Idiot?"

The man still stared.

"Yes, it's my way of calling you an idiot," said Alice, noticing sparks of angry understanding light up in the man's eyes.

He moved toward her, drunk, determined, and threatening. Instinctively, Alice stepped back and Vlad appeared between them, face to face with the mustached man.

"You came to the wrong place, buddy," Vlad said, stopping the drunkard.

Three guards now appeared and surrounded the man. He did not resist them as his aggressiveness suddenly subsided into a pitiful whine.

"I came to the wrong place? I? She left me without a penny, and now she sells my art collection. My art collection!" he yelled to the crowd before guards led him out of the garden.

People whispered and exchanged meaningful looks. Alice and Vlad stood facing each other.

"Do you know the story behind this?" Alice asked.

"I do and it's an ugly one," he answered. "I would tell you, but only if you agree to come with me."

"Come with you?"

"It's my birthday today, and my younger sister arranged a surprise party, which I presumably know nothing about. Now I have to come home and act all surprised. I think I'll be more convincing if I come home with a beautiful lady. My sister would be delighted to think that she caught me at such a moment."

"That's an interesting setup. But I don't think it's a good idea."

"Come on. There's nothing left to do here anyway. And I wouldn't have to be bored at my own birthday party."

"No. I'm tired and my feet hurt. I'd rather go home tonight."

* * *

Alice gave Vlad her correct phone number but refused to take his. She said, "If you want to call me, you will."

Vlad called her the next evening.

"I remembered something important," he said instead of introductions.

"And what is that?" asked Alice, unsure whom she was speaking with.

"You said that you must be asked several times before you can say yes. So how about a dinner date after work?"

Alice laughed. She said yes.

Charmer had to save the butterfly from the hungry bird and now wished to guard her from any hunter that might follow. Before she knew it, she was entangled in gentle web strings of Charmer's beard. It was nothing like a spider web since it did not hurt her in the least. The butterfly could leave and enjoy the summer morning on her own.

Yet she was entangled because she always missed Charmer and had to come back. Some butterflies spend their lifetimes fluttering from one flower to another, forever restless and homeless. Others perish from birds and spiders. How difficult it is to know the difference between the spider web and Charmer's beard before being caught by one or the other. No intelligence, no beauty can assist in this matter. It is only fate that unites the butterfly with her Charmer.

Soon the evening came when Alice agreed to stay over at Vlad's apartment. The anticipation, the fear locked her throat and she was unable to pronounce a word. But she did not want him to stop. She had awaited this night for so long.

Alice was forever thankful to the voice, his arousing voice that guided her into his arms, undressed her, excited her. Charmer kissed her wings apart, but she panicked and ran to another room. Alice was forever thankful that he went after her and carried her back. Once more he caressed her wings. His voice charmed Alice with his admiration of her beauty. He described the titillating details of colorful ornaments, painting them on her wings. She never knew anything like the images his voice created. The butterfly cannot color her own wings and for many years Alice held hers closed, prohibiting anyone else from marking them up. Once more, Charmer kissed her wings apart and they flew together, uniting the man with the woman, the dream with reality, the notion with the object, the images with words, with actions.

* * *

**ButterCat**

*(Hypolimnas dexithea/Madagascar)*

* * *

Once the novelty faded, Vlad grew disappointed with Alice. She was far too reserved, too shy in her lovemaking. Still, she was interesting to have in his life and so the relationship dragged on.

Next summer, Alice convinced Vlad to take a two-week vacation and visit her homeland. Entering the overseas village, Vlad found himself in another world, the world that he recognized in Alice, the world that made her so unique. How dearly she loved it. How dear and special she became to Vlad during those few days of their stay.

Together they went gathering raspberries in the forest. It was an unusually hot day and Vlad unbuttoned his shirt. The swarm of mosquitoes prevented him from taking it off altogether. Alice chatted away, recalling various stories from her childhood. Then she looked up from the raspberry bush and stopped talking right in the middle of the sentence. She stared at Vlad with the mischievous smile that did not belong to her familiar reservoir of expressions. Alice came near him and touched her lips to his bare chest, licking his skin with her tongue. Then she raised her head and spat a mosquito onto the ground.

Another mosquito appeared before their eyes and Alice did not move, allowing it to settle on the elevation of her breast, which showed in her unbuttoned blouse. Vlad pinned it with his tongue and decided to swallow it, bringing absolute delight to his partner's face. Dropping their baskets to the ground, they entwined and united in a passionate lovemaking that Alice had instigated herself for the first time. That day they came back without the raspberries, and their bodies itched with mosquito bites.

Alice began surprising him, lifting him to new heights of ecstasy with her fantasies. It was as though she needed permission from Lisa, permission from her village, from her childhood to enter into the adult world where age alone could not take her. She was granted that permission and could now be Vlad's Charmer as much as he was hers. She was ready to accept the crown she was once denied many years ago. All this time she searched for her Charmer and now became one herself. Now she had the powers to preside over the Festival of Farces, to play and to trick, never compromising the grace and the kindness, never leaving her partner lost in the magical woods, never forgetting the importance of leading him home when the game was over.

Charmer walks through the forest.

Printed in the United States
206748BV00001B/106-159/P